MOUNTAIN RIDERS

Max Brand

Another great adventure story of the
legendary Silvertip and his struggle
with the master outlaw, Barry
Christian. To return a favor, Tom
Derry helped Christian escape from
jail and became a hunted man.
Silvertip showed him his mistake
and Derry swore to get the outlaw,
at the cost of his life.

MAX BRAND WESTERNS
IN LARGE PRINT

THE BIG TRAIL

DAN BARRY'S DAUGHTER

MOUNTAIN RIDERS

MAX BRAND

Mountain Riders

John Curley & Associates, Inc.
South Yarmouth, Ma.

1

Tom Derry

Tom Derry was not a handsome man. He was rather tall and very lean, and the narrows of his waist ran up almost to his shoulders, and one had to look twice to see where his hips appeared. But his appearance was deceptive, for his leanness was twisted about with muscles like hard fingers of wisteria that intertwine around the trunk of an old tree.

His face was no better-looking than his scrawny body. He had a nose, but that was about all one could say for it. He had plenty of mouth. He had a blunt jaw of the sort that does not telegraph the shock of blows against the base of the brain. In fact, he had what is generally called a "mug," but his eyes were so bright and good-humoured and active, and his smile was such a genuine flash of happiness that people always put him down as a harmless sort.

That had been the wrecking of Tom

Derry's life, so far. Because there was a time when all the good nature in him was exhausted, and his grin was not one of pleasure, and his eyes were a blue fire. A good many people had discovered that second half of Tom's being, but most of those who made the discovery went to the hospital for quite a period, and long before they came out, Tom Derry had found it advisable to move on.

He kept on moving.

He had grown up on the range as easily, as carelessly, as naturally as the grama-grass and the wild-eyed cattle that grazed on it. Then, in the midst of a little friendly wrestling bout, a Mexican lad had pulled a knife on Derry and had seen the smile of Tom turn into the battle grin. Derry broke the Mexican's arm, got the knife, and used it.

The Mexican did not die, but Tom thought he would. He lighted out from the home and dived into the wilderness and came up in a lumber camp, far north, where he worked happily until a peevish Canuck one day threw an axe at him. Tom pulled the axe out of the tree in which its blade was buried and threw it right back at the Canuck – and hit his mark.

The Canuck did not die, in fact, but Tom never knew that. He dived into the wilderness again and came to the surface in a town far east and south, where he drove a delivery wagon for a butcher's shop until a pair of town toughs decided to help themselves to some steaks across the tailboard of the wagon. Tom took a cleaver, dealt with them, and moved on again.

He worked on the streets; he became a tramp; he did a few shifts in a coal-mine; he finally felt that he had achieved the really free and noble life that is proper for a man when he signed aboard a tramp freighter which used sail and a crew of Swedes. The Swedes did not like Derry because he was not a Swede. They started to ride him, and they rode him all the way to Acapulco. There he threw off the load, and in the fall three Swedish heads were broken.

Derry left the ship and drifted north through Mexico until he found a job as a vaquero. There he endured, happily, until a Mexican caballero turned the edge of his knife on Derry's skull; but the knife still had a point, and Tom drove that point between the greaser's ribs, and moved north, by night.

So, at the age of twenty-two, he got off

3

his mustang and stood in Cleve Walker's saloon, hankering for nothing more than beer for his stomach and peace for his soul.

Walker's place was cool. The floor had been sloshed down recently with buckets of water. A mist was still rising from the boards. The saloon was so dim and calm that one lowered the voice instinctively on entering. Derry had lowered his voice, though he always spoke quietly enough. Now he stood at the bar, and with his finger-tips caressed the frost on the outside of his glass of beer, and was thankful that he was safely out of Mexico.

All he wanted was more safety – and a little beer. All he wanted the rest of his life was peace, perfect peace. He could almost envy dead men, they were so peaceful.

So he dropped his head back a little – which made his neck look broken at the adam's apple – and sipped his beer, and smiled dreamily on the bartender.

When he opened his eyes wide, he saw, on the wall above the bar, a big white placard that carried in the centre the photograph of a man with a long moustache and deadly, dull, expressionless eyes. Underneath the picture there was the terrible caption, "Wanted. For Murder,"

4

and then, "Twenty-five Hundred Dollars Reward." And there was some more of the usual stuff – the description – information leading to the apprehension – and that sort of thing.

Derry shook his head, still staring at that picture.

"The fool!" he said softly.

There were other men at the bar. One of them wore his shirt open half-way down his chest. He was a red man. His hair was red. His face was red. His uncropped beard was red. The backs of his hands were blistered red. He was built like a buffalo bull, with a hump of strength across his shoulders.

"What fool?" asked this gentleman.

"Stan Parker, take it easy," cautioned the bartender.

But red Stan Parker wanted trouble. He always wanted trouble. He never had had enough of it to suit him.

"That fool," Tom Derry was saying. "That one in the picture. Murder! Any man that does a murder, he's just a fool!"

"You wouldn't do a murder, I guess?" asked Stan Parker grimly.

"Me? I'd run a thousand miles first," said Derry. He sighed and shook his head slowly from side to side. "I'd walk ten

5

miles and swim a river to get out of the way of a fight."

There was something about the hearty, the soul-convincing way in which he said this, that might have given a reasonable man pause for thought, but Stan Parker was not reasonable, and he was not interested in thinking. Action was all he knew and it was all that he liked.

"Suppose that hombre up there in the picture got in a jam and had to fight his way out?" suggested Parker.

"It's the worst way in the world, I'll tell a man," said Derry. "Don't talk to me! It's the worst way."

He shook his head again, and sipped his beer.

"It ain't no particular privilege to talk to you," declared Parker.

"Now, Stan!" said the bartender soothingly.

But the other men in the saloon began to prick up their ears and turn their faces, and their eyes were shining a little as they looked toward trouble. They were a reasonably tough lot, and they liked to see a fight.

"I was sayin'," repeated Parker, when he knew that he had the attention of his

6

audience, "that it ain't no particular privilege to talk to you."

"Sure it isn't," agreed Tom Derry. "I never said it was." He glanced at Stan Parker, and then added: "Hey, don't come around here looking for any trouble, because you won't get any out of me. I'll run first."

"Just plain yaller, are you?" commented Parker, drawing back half a step from this monster among men.

"Oh, I dunno," said Tom Derry. "You know how it is. I don't want any trouble. That's all."

"I don't know how it is," said Parker. The bully in him made his mouth water. He came closer to his victim.

"Look," said Tom Derry, "if you want me out of the way, I'll go out of the way. Mind that? I'll run away, if I have to, to get out of trouble. Only – don't crowd me!"

As he said that, he set his teeth, and a cord stood out from the base of his jaw all the way down to his collarbone, and his mouth stretched in a grin that was mirthless.

"I ain't to crowd you, eh?" said Stan Parker.

"Aw, let me finish this beer, and I'll get

7

out," said Tom Derry.

He raised the glass to his lips.

"What I wanta know," said Parker, in argumentative fashion, "is how come you got the right to call a gent a fool – a gent like that one hangin' on the wall? You know him?"

"He did a murder. That's why he's a fool," said Tom Derry. "That's all I know about him."

"That's a hell of a lot, ain't it? Why, there's times when a gent would be a skunk, if he didn't fight – with guns! And if he's lucky, he's called a murderer; and if he ain't lucky, he's dead. So what you goin' to do about it?"

"I'm going to get out of this place," said Tom Derry. "That's what I'm going to do about it."

"Oh, you're goin' to get out, are you?" queried Parker. "I dunno, though. When you leave here, maybe you're goin' to take something with you to remember your manners by."

He stood still closer. He was big, and he loomed higher than Tom Derry. He could have been split in two down the middle, and each half of him would have made the bulk of another Tom Derry. The sense of his size comforted the fighting heart of Stan Parker.

"A sneakin' yaller-belly," said Stan, "who comes around here and starts damning folks that he never laid his eyes on. That's what kind of sickens me. That's what I'm goin' to do something about. I dunno how you got the face to talk. Lemme see what kind of a face you got."

He took Tom Derry by the point of the chin and pulled his head around and looked down into Derry's mug.

"You ain't got no kind of a face to please me," said Parker.

"Take your hand off my chin," said Derry gently. "Please take it off, mister. I want to finish my beer!"

"The devil with you and your beer!" shouted Parker, the cruel passion suddenly roaring out of his throat. "I'm goin' to kick you out into the gutter!"

He laid his hand on the nape of Derry's neck. But then a blunt weapon struck upward against the point of Parker's chin. It knocked a shower of sparks out of the top of his head. It sent him backward until his shoulders bumped heavily against the wall.

"Well, by thunder!" groaned Parker, and put down his head, and launched

9

himself, and rushed across the floor of the saloon. He simply ran his chin into a stone wall that was otherwise called a straight left. It bumped him to a stop – a full stop.

"I don't want any trouble. Take him off me, some of you, will you?" pleaded Tom Derry. "I just want to finish my beer."

He actually stepped to the bar and took a hasty swallow.

"Has he got you licked, Stan? Are you drunk?" shouted someone to the bully. For the prowess of Stan Parker with his hands was known as far as the mountains.

"Him? I'm – I'm goin' to tear the dirty black-jack in two!" shouted Stan, and came in again.

He came more cautiously and properly, patting the floor before him with his left foot, and sneaking the right foot in from behind, as every good boxer ought to do. He had his guard raised properly, he was beautifully balanced, and out of that balance he rammed a fist at the head of Tom Derry.

"I don't want any trouble! I won't fight! Take him away!" Derry was crying, when that punch landed on the point of his durable chin. The weight of the blow folded him back over the edge of the bar. A

10

pair of hands gripped his throat.

And then something happened. Tom Derry hardly knew what it was. He only knew that the old red madness had burned up in his mind like a flame. He only knew that he was striking out, and that his fists were sinking into a soft body, or hammering on a hard skull.

Then there was nothing before him, but on the floor crouched Stan Parker. Stan was redder than ever, now. The good crimson of his blood was swiped over his face in masses. Some of it dripped off his chin. He was beaten. He was frightened. And the savage was, therefore, raging in him. Around the room, he saw grinning, well-contented faces. Suddenly he knew that it was better to be hanged than so shamed.

"You sneakin' ringer!" screamed Stan Parker, and pulled out a .45.

He fired. The bullet went where Tom Derry had been, but Tom had leaped high and aside, like a mongoose. He landed right on Stan Parker. They rolled over and over. The gun exploded again. Then Derry pushed the limp body aside and rose to his feet. He looked sick. A smear of Parker's blood across his forehead made him seem

11

horribly pale.

"Somebody take a look," he said. "See if he's dead. I'm – I can't touch him again."

2

A Scrap Of Paper

Stan Parker was not beloved. He had made his way through the world as a man makes his way through a wall – by constant hammering. Now the men in the saloon gathered around the loosely lying body and made comments, regardless of how young Tom Derry stood at the bar with his chin dropped on one fist.

Tom Derry stared into the mirror and saw his own face and told himself that that face was no good.

Vaguely he heard the men talking behind him.

"I guess he's ticked off."

"Yeah, when they got their eyes just a little open like that and their mouth open, too – just like they was goin' to wake up and start takin' – that's when you tell they're done in."

"It's their eyes. When their eyes look like dead fish, then you tell."

13

"A doctor had oughta come and pronounce him dead," said the bartender, putting his hands on his knees and leaning over the man.

"He don't need no doctor pronouncin' nothin'," said another. "He's dead as anything. The kid split his wishbone for him."

"I ought to run," said Tom Derry to himself. "But to hell with running. I'm tired of running. Better for white men to hang me than lascars or greasers, or something."

After a few moments, the sheriff came in. He was a man with a fat stomach, and a golden watch-fob hanging out of his vest pocket. He wore no coat. His sleeves were held up by elastic garters, red and blue, worn around the fat of his arm. He pulled up a chair and sat down by the corpse. He made a cigarette and dribbled the tobacco over the body and even on the face of Stan.

"Sure he's dead," said the sheriff, lifting a leg and scratching a match on the tight under-surface of his pants. "He's dead as last Wednesday's fish. The big, red-faced bum! I'm glad he's gone. Who done it? The kid there? Self-defense, wasn't it, kid?"

Tom Derry said nothing. He kept

looking at himself in the mirror. He kept hating himself.

"The kid's sick at the stomach," said the sheriff. "A lot of gents get that way when they see blood all over the floor. Give him a shot of whisky, Cleve."

"He won't take none," said Cleve. "It was self-defense, all right. The kid didn't want – "

"Aw, sure, sure," said the sheriff. "Sure it was self-defense. It would be self-defense, in this town, if somebody had plugged Stan right through the back. The big, red-headed bum! What a lot quieter things are goin' to be now! Kid, you goin' to bury the victim? No, you let it go. The whole town'll contribute. We'll dig the grave deep, too. What a yaller pack we been to let Stan stick around so long, anyway!"

Tom Derry listened to these calm remarks with very little satisfaction. Now that he was tired of running away from the results of his battles, it seemed that men no longer wish to hunt him. He could not understand this. He was baffled, and almost unhappy. His mind was not functioning very clearly, for the moment.

When he turned around, the sheriff had

15

put a bandanna over the face of Stan Parker, and had taken everything out of his pockets and piled it on a table. There was not a great deal. There was something over two hundred dollars in cash, and a pocket-knife, tobacco, papers, matches, some string, a little coil of bailing wire, some odds and ends, a note-book, and three very soiled envelopes.

A little rag of paper blew off the table and dropped to the floor, and Tom Derry picked it up.

"What's that you got, kid?" asked the sheriff.

"Aw, just a scrap," said Derry, staring down at it.

"There's enough money here to bury Stan," said the sheriff cheerfully, "and to buy drinks all around, too. Set up the drinks, Cleve. Stan can rest just as well inside a pine coffin as he could in solid silver. And we'll spend all the change in a few rounds of drinks. Come on, boys. Step up! Step up! Here's to the kid. Long may he wave! A game youngster, he is, and he scavenged this here town for us. Here's to the kid, and bottoms up. Hey, where is the kid, anyway?"

The "kid" was already out, through a

16

side door, and had taken his mustang and ridden down the first alley off the main street. He put the bronco into a canter and kept at that pace until he was well outside of the town, and there he drew rein and pulled a scrap of paper from his pocket.

There were not many words. It was just the lower part of a sheet of ordinary correspondence paper, and across it was written:

– your share in the business. It's a big thing, and we ought to do it. Meet me in Thompson's Creek, by the split rock, as fast as you can come. This is going to be the turning point in your life, Stan. If you will only –

Young Tom Derry read the words through again, the paper flapping up and down as the horse jogged along. He had a very strange feeling that that paper had blown to his feet for a mysterious reason. He had a feeling, too, that in the one case where people had not driven him, after he had done a killing, he would now be hounded by the soul of the dead man himself. He thought of the red face and the cruel eyes of Stan Parker and shuddered. But, after all, he knew that all through his being there was a response, as if to a command. Into Stan Parker's shoes he intended to step and keep the rendezvous for the dead man.

3

The Red Bull

It took Derry five days to get to Thompson's Creek, for it was 'way up in the Blue Water Mountains. It took him two days of wandering about through Thompson's Creek before a travelling cowpuncher gave him the location of the split rock. It was not a very big affair. It was no larger, say, than a small house, and it was cleft right in two, with the halves leaning quite away from one another and looking as though they would fall utterly apart.

He was vigorously introduced to the scene by a red bull. The bull had scars along its flanks which proved that it had been thrashed by a rival not long before, and had been gored before it could dodge away from the conqueror. And there was a store of malice lodged in its heart that sent it high-tailing straight for the rider.

Tom Derry dodged that bull twice. If it

had not been a splendid specimen he would have been tempted to shoot it down, but as it was, he made the pony run to save his life.

The worst of that manœuvre was that the moment the mustang started running, it fell into a panic, and headed blindly for a high, barbed-wire fence. Tom Derry managed to twist the mustang aside from that terrible danger, but the horse seemed to think that its master was holding it so that the bull could catch up from the rear.

So it tied itself in two or three figure eights, double-bucked a few jumps, and plastered Tom Derry against the barbed-wire fence.

There was no particular malice in that horse, and if Tom had been a bit more on his guard, the bronco probably would not have got him off. But as it was, he hung head down on the fence, with only a blurred realization that the red bull was plunging straight at him, head lowered.

The head dropped still lower. The bull dug its horns into the ground and turned a complete somersault, barely missing the body of Derry with its flinging heels. Then it lay still, and Derry vaguely realized that he had heard the report of a rifle in the distance.

He got a good many deep scratches before he managed to disentangle himself from the fence. Then, standing up, he saw a rider cantering toward him – still a good two hundred yards away!

Derry looked at the bull and saw where the little rifle bullet had bored to the life through the shoulder. It had been a neat shot; a snap shot and an excellent one. Derry, with the world of blue and bright still spinning a little before his eyes, realized that his life had been saved.

He turned from the bull and found the rider dismounting beside him from a tall black mare that had all the long, stretching lines of good blood. He was a man of fifty perhaps, with a face heavily but pleasantly lined, a long-legged fellow with a rather studious humping of the shoulders. He wore a checkered shirt, a very clean bandanna about his neck, and the finest of shop-made boots with spoon-handled spurs on his heels. Little golden bells made music on those spurs.

Derry went up to him and held out his hand.

"My name is Derry," he said. "There wouldn't be any Derry if you didn't think as fast as you shoot straight. Thanks!"

"It's a queer thing about red bulls," said the stranger. "You don't have to bait 'em. They go mad with their own colour, I suppose."

He chuckled a little as he said this. His eyes, under their wrinkled lids, moved quickly up and down Derry, appraised him, registered him in a mental file with other men.

"He's not some of your own beef?" asked Derry courteously.

"None of mine. I don't live in this part of the world," said the stranger. "I've been looking for a rider that you may have seen on your way. Big red man. Red hair. Mostly unshaven. Looks as though the sun were cooking him and swelling him up."

Derry stared.

"You mean Stan Parker?" he asked, and saw the name strike the other with a shock.

"Have you come from Parker?" asked the stranger sharply.

"I've come in his place – if I'll do," said Derry.

"That's strange!"

A lie, to Derry, was something that came very hard. He looked straight at the other and then said:

"I'll tell you how it came about. There was a brawl down the line. Parker was pretty abusive. We got into a fight. He pulled a gun. I killed him with his own gun."

He stopped and waited. He saw the glance of the other wavering over him again, in an entirely new appraisal.

"Stan was always a bully," said the stranger.

"They called it self-defense. They laid him out and went through his pockets. Off the table where the stuff was laid, this scrap of paper blew across the floor to me."

He handed the scrap to the stranger.

"And it seemed to me," said Derry, "that the best thing I could do was to try to make up for killing Parker by showing up here."

"Well," said the stranger, "this is one of those queer stories. But I believe you. What did you intend to do when you got here?"

"Did you ever kill a man?" asked Derry bluntly.

"Nothing I'd ever like to think about," came the evasive answer.

"I've had bad luck," said Derry. "I haven't carried a gun or a knife for three

23

years. But in spite of that, I've had piles of bad luck. And here's one life that I'd like to carry on a few steps along the way it would have gone, except for me."

"You mean," said the other, "that you're not packing a gun at this minute?"

"Nor a knife."

"And yet you tell a man who expects to meet Parker that you killed Stan?"

"You mean, it might have made you draw on me?"

"That's what I mean," said the stranger coldly.

"No," said Derry, "you may know him, but you're not a friend of Parker's."

"What makes you think I'm not?"

"You're a big cut above him."

"This is the damnest thing I've ever heard of."

"You wanted Parker for something. A hired man, I suppose. Well, it looks as though you've hired me and paid me in advance."

Derry pointed toward the dead bull, whose tongue lolled out in the dust.

"You're named Derry, are you?" asked the stranger.

"Yes."

"I've never heard of you."

"I'm new to this part of the world," Derry told him. "I've been out of the West, mostly, for six or seven years."

"Clear out?"

"As clear as Shanghai – and farther."

The stranger shook his head. At last he said: "Come over and sit in the shade with me."

They went over and sat in the shade of the split rock, after Derry had caught his frightened mustang.

After that, a silence settled down on the two men, and the scratching of matches and the lighting of cigarettes did not lead to conversation at once. Outside the meagre shadow that fell over them, the sun poured incessant fire on the summer-whitened grass, and the heat reflected in shimmering waves. Off in the distance was the playing sound of Thompson's Creek, a thread of coolness in the warmth of the day. And a sense of unreality came over Tom Derry. He found himself looking again and again toward the carcass of the red bull in the next field. He stared up, and saw buzzards coming. One was already circling low. Out of the distance more of them were coming, little spots in the pallor of the sky.

"I've got to find the owner of that bull,"

25

said Derry. "I've got to make a deal with him, and pay – part of the price anyway."

"Pay him for having a bull that nearly killed you?" said the stranger.

"It was my fault – letting the mustang pitch me off."

"You don't aim to slide out from under the trouble that comes your way?"

"You know how it is," said Derry, sighing. "The fellow you dodge today gets you coming around the corner tomorrow."

"Humph!" said the stranger. He added suddenly: "My name is Rainey. Buck Rainey."

He seemed to be waiting, with a rather stiff expectancy.

"I never heard of you," answered Derry. "Sorry!"

"I'm not so sorry. It's all right, I mean. You mean, really, that you don't know people in this part of the world? You ride like a real puncher."

"I was raised on the range. Nine years ago I got off it. I haven't been on many parts of it since. Are you a rancher around here, Mr. Rainey?"

"I've done ranching, too," said Rainey, musingly, and his side glance flickered brightly at Derry again. "You've been away

26

so long that all you know about the West is Jim Silver?" he suggested.

"Silver? That's a queer name."

"Hello! You never heard of him?"

"Never that I know of," said Derry. "It's a strange enough name to remember, too."

"Nor of Barry Christian?"

"No. Nor Barry Christian. Christian? No, I've never heard of him, either. What are they? Senators, or something like that?"

"No," said Buck Rainey, laughing. "Not senators, either. But Barry Christian is a friend of mine," he added with a sudden solemnity.

He waited again, as though certain to hear some comment. Derry was merely silent, nodding, expectant of more.

"I sent for Stan Parker," went on Rainey, "because I had to have a man I could trust on an important errand. And Stan could be trusted – by people he was afraid of. That's true of a good many bullies. I needed a man badly. And – "

Here he paused to resume his survey of Derry.

"There's the price you paid for me," said Derry, pointing again to the dead bull.

27

"Neither Silver nor Christian!" muttered Rainey.

"No, I never heard of either of them."

"Well," said Rainey, shrugging his shoulders, "I'll have to do a lot of explaining then."

Derry raised his hand.

"You don't have to explain to me," he declared. "Whatever you tell me to do is good enough for me. I – never owed anything to any man before today. I want to clear the score away."

"I believe you," answered Rainey, very seriously and gravely. "I'll only explain this. My friend Christian is a badly misunderstood man. Have you ever been misunderstood yourself?"

"Have I? Yes. With the butt end of a blacksnake I've been misunderstood." Derry chuckled to himself.

"Some people have even accused you of murder?"

Derry made a gesture with both hands, as he answered: "I've been chased out of half a dozen countries, if that's what you mean!"

"The fact is," said Rainey, "that I'm telling you about as fine a gentleman as ever sat in a saddle or pulled a right in a fight. A

28

man, Derry, who has been misunderstood and persecuted by the world because of the dirty misrepresentations of a scoundrel; a man who has been hunted into prison by the same hypocrite and sneak; and a man who is in danger of hanging within a few days because the same devil has hounded him into trouble."

"Who?" exclaimed Tom Derry. "Rainey, when I hear you talk like this, I've *got* to take a hand!"

"You're made of the right stuff," said Rainey. "I think at your age I would have been keen as steel to get into this sort of a game. But the thing I want to do is a terrible hard thing, Derry. I want to save my friend's life. I want to get him out of prison."

"Ay," said Derry cheerfully, and his bright blue eyes sparkled as he looked at Rainey. "You're the sort of a man who would want to do that, Rainey. You wouldn't let a friend down."

"But it's a hard job. Because the sheriff knows that Christian has friends, and he's taking every precaution to keep Christian well guarded. He's gone so far that he's found a set of men who hate Christian — because the wool was pulled over their eyes

29

by that same fiend of a Jim Silver. Those men he's using to guard Christian in the jail at Blue Water. Do you understand?"

"That sounds like spite."

"Spite? Jim Silver has poured every man's mind full of hate for Barry Christian. An outrage, Derry."

"Ah," said Derry, "I'd like to put hands on that fellow Silver."

"Never mind him. Wait till we can wrangle Christian out of jail. I say that the sheriff has hired the toughest fellows he can find, and that's a whole clan called Cary, Ever hear of them?"

"I don't think so."

"You'll hear of them some day, though. They can't be kept down, and they can't be kept out of mind. Oh, you'll hear from them, well enough. A hard, strong gang, Derry. And this is my idea. The sheriff trusts the Cary clan to guard Christian. And Silver trusts the Cary outfit to keep Christian till he's hung. Now, then, suppose that I could bribe the Cary men — you see? I'd take everyone by surprise and have poor Barry out of the jail!"

"I see. Yes, that's clear enough."

"But I can't get near the Carys. I can't go down into the town of Blue Water at all —

because I'm one of the men that that devil Silver lied about. I'd be shot at sight. I'd be thrown into the jail along with my friend Christian!"

"That's why you need a messenger?"

"A messenger to carry twenty-five thousand dollars into Cary Valley, see Old Man Cary, and make a bargain with him. A messenger that I can trust with that much of a treasure."

"Rainey," said Derry, much moved, "you love your friend, poor Barry Christian!"

"I think more of him than of anyone else," said Rainey simply.

"Then," said Derry, "there's no use talking. If he means so much to you, I'll do anything to get Christian free for you!"

4

Good Shooting

Rainey said it would be harder for him to pass through Blue Water than for a camel to pass through the eye of a needle, and he smiled a little when he said this. He had a way of smiling somewhat askance at his own words and ideas, as though he found his ideas petty things and would forgive another person for passing them over with a shrug of the shoulders.

It was very plain to Derry that his companion was different from other men. His background was not that which one would expect to encounter on the range, and when they caught trout out of Thompson's Creek and broiled them for a lunch, he noticed that Rainey ate with a care as meticulous and a propriety as great as though he had been seated at a table in a fashionable restaurant. He had a little knife and fork set, and putting his portion of the trout on the clean inside of bark, he removed the bones dexterously and balanced the bark on one knee while he ate slowly. He even had a collapsible cup for his coffee, which he sipped while he ate, and he kept up a mild stream of conversation through the meal.

Tom Derry was more accustomed to the manners of forecastles and cook wagons. He wolfed his portion, swallowed his coffee, and then lay on his back under a tree and smoked, and stared at his companion with a good deal of relish.

"Listen, Rainey," he broke in at last, "I don't want to seem curious, or ask questions, but I suppose that you've stepped around in some pretty steep and lofty places. You didn't dig all your lingo out of funny papers and the fifth reader. You've been through college and stayed a while. Am I wrong?"

"I've had a chance to learn a good deal from books," said Rainey, "but I've never learned the thing that I need to know now."

"What's that?" asked Derry.

"How to handle a six-shooter like Jim Silver."

"He's good, is he?"

"I understand that he's about the best in

the world. How are you with a gun, my friend?"

"Lend me yours, and I'll show you," said Derry.

It was a good new Colt, and Tom Derry stood up and looked about him for a target. He selected a sapling with a six-inch trunk, about twenty steps away, and fired at it three times. One bullet missed, one clipped the rim, one slogged right into the heart of the little tree.

"That's not so bad," said Tom Derry. "I can do much better than that when I'm in good practice, though."

"Throw the gun back to me," suggested Rainey.

Derry handed the Colt, instead of throwing it. And he saw Rainey swing the gun carelessly over his knee and flick the hammer three times with his thumb. The gun jerked rapidly with explosions. Right around the bull's-eye that Derry had made appeared three spots, quite regularly placed.

"Great thunder!" cried Derry. "You could shoot the eyes out of a man at that rate!"

"I'm only a novice and a beginner compared with Barry Christian, and he's left-handed compared with Jim Silver. The thing for you to do, Derry, is to keep away from gunmen in this part of the country. If you're going to try to get to Cary Valley for me, don't start any fights."

"They're born with knives in their teeth and guns in their hands, are they?" asked Derry.

"Pretty much that way," replied Rainey.

"Well," said Derry, "If I shoot slower, I'll shoot straighter."

"If you shoot slower, you'll die in a shower of lead," Rainey warned.

"Maybe. But the other fellow's going to die with me. I can be slow enough to be sure, all right."

Rainey remarked: "Good shooting is good shooting, Derry."

"And a fight is always a fight," answered Derry.

Rainey pulled out a leather case that was filled with long, thin cigars and offered one to Derry, who refused.

"Those are too good for me," said Derry.

"What makes you think they're good," asked Rainey.

"There was a look in your face, when you offered them to me, as though you had your heart in your hand."

"I'm sorry, and you're welcome to one."

"I'll drink your best whisky when you're at home," said Derry calmly. "But out on the range, every man ought to have a chance to enjoy the stuff he packs with him."

"You're a philosopher," said Rainey, biting off the end of his cigar with his white teeth. "Where have you been educated, Tom?"

"I went to a country school three days a week, for three or four whole winters," said Derry. "And I picked up a lot of facts on the street and on the bum and before the mast. You know how it is. I got through a lot of grades, but it's the sort of a school that you never graduate from."

"I know." Rainey smiled as he lighted his cigar and began to smoke it tenderly. "But you use good English. How does that happen?"

"I sailed a couple of years," said Derry, "with a red-nosed, hard-handed, whisky soak as skipper of the ship. He was a Yankee and he'd been through all sorts of colleges. He used to go on a binge two or three times a week, unless we were lying off the Horn or making land, and the day after he'd had a bust, he was pretty shaky. The only thing that quieted him down and rubbed the edges off his sharp nerves was reading aloud. He picked me for the job. A lot of times when the rest of the boys were washing decks, or making sail, or doing any of the kind of dirt that comes your way at sea, the skipper would have me in his cabin reading to him. And every time I mispronounced a word, he'd put me right. And if I mispronounced the same word twice, he'd be apt to get up and come for me. He was six-feet-something and two hundred pounds of hell. He used to beat me to a pulp until I learned how to box from fighting him."

"A hard way to learn," said Rainey, smiling.

"A fast way, and a good way," answered Derry. "A right hook that knocks you flat every time it socks you is a punch that you learn to block. The skipper's jaw was so hard that I broke my hand the first time I hit it. That taught me how to grip my hands. You can knock the edge off a block of stone, if you hold your hands right."

"What became of the skipper?" asked Rainey.

"Oh, it's a long story. He rode the men

so long that they threw him over the side into a boat, one day, and they threw me after him, and we lived on rain-water and fish, now and then, for thirty days before we made land. And the skipper was so tired of water that when we made port, he went on a ten-day binge that finished him. I planted him down there in Valparaiso and came north again."

Rainey nodded. He took out a wallet and from it counted out a stack of bills. He pushed the money out to Derry.

"That's twenty-five thousand dollars," he said. "Maybe you can get to Old Man Cary, and maybe you can buy him for less than that amount. If you can, you'll get a cut of what you save."

Derry took the sheaf of bills and smoothed them carefully. He sighed. A little shudder ran through him.

"I'm not worrying," said Rainey. "That stuff will be safe with you. It's going to be all right."

Derry grinned. "It's going to be tough to go straight where you're sending me," he said. "But I'll see what I can do for you. When do I start?"

"Now," said Rainey. "I'll take you as far along the way as I can."

5

Another Debt

They spent that day and most of the next riding steadily north and west through the foothills, through the lower mountains, and the second afternoon they came down a long gully with a bit of a town stuck in the middle of it.

"It's getting close to Blue Water," said Rainey. It's getting so close that it may be a bad chance for me to try to ride through that town down there. But we waste two or three hours if we cut around it."

"You mean to say that if the people spot you, they'll open up with guns?" asked Derry. "Isn't there any law up here?"

"There's no law in the Blue Waters," said Rainey. He waved his hand towards the great sweep of the mountains. "Nothing but hawks and eagles fly this high," he explained, "and the same crook who put Barry Christian in jail knows how to get the crooks and the roughs on his side.

39

In every prison in the United States, the lifers and the long-termers talk about this hole-in-the-wall and try to get here if they can make a break. No wonder Jim Silver is able to build up a following!"

"I've got a feeling," said Tom Derry, "that my grip would just fit snug around his throat."

But Rainey said, shaking his head: "Never you mix with Jim Silver. He's as big as your Yankee skipper, and he's a lot faster and stronger."

"You never saw that skipper," said Derry.

"And you never saw Silver. The difference between him and other men is the difference between a hundred-and-fifty-pound dog and a hundred-and-fifty-pound cat. I've seen him dissolve three big, hard-handed roughs like three spoonfuls of sugar in a cup of tea. No, no, don't be that ambitious. Don't mix with Jim Silver!"

Derry sighed and nodded again.

"All right," he said. "I won't mix with him then. What does he look like?"

"He's easily spotted. He carries himself like a king. By his head and his big shoulders you can spot him, for one thing, and if he takes off his hat, you'll see a

40

couple of tufts of silver-grey hair over the temples, like horns that are beginning to sprout. But don't ask questions about him. You'll find that nine-tenths of these crooks, up here, believe in Silver. He's paid for that belief. And if you ask questions of them, they'll start asking questions of *you*."

"I'll keep my mouth shut," said Derry. "It seems sort of queer, though. That's all."

"The Blue Waters are the home of queer things," said Rainey. "But we'll ride down the valley here and see if we can slip through the town."

They rode down the gorge, therefore, dipping out of the sunlight into the warm shadow that filled the ravine, and so they came into the little town that sprawled its unpainted shacks right and left of the trail as carelessly as any town in all the casual West.

They came to the general merchandise store, where the usual line of loungers were tilted back in their chairs, sleepy-looking men with cigarettes drawling out of the corners of their unshaven lips. They were almost past when there was a loud Indian yell, and then:

"Get 'em boys! It's Buck Rainey! Get

41

'em!"

Buck Rainey flattened himself along the back of his mount, and the black went away like the wind.

The mustang of Tom Derry, however, had no mind to run until a rifle bullet clipped off the top of one ear. Then it went away like mad, and Derry, looking back, saw the pursuit sweeping after him – three, four, a dozen riders in varying groups as they managed to scramble out of houses and into saddles, roused by the yelling that echoed up and down the street, and the roaring of gun-fire.

Derry was not three jumps up the winding trail beyond the town, with Rainey out of sight before him, and only a hanging ghost of dust to show where the long-legged black mare had vanished, before it was clear that there were better animals, by far, in the pursuit, than the bronco under Derry's saddle.

Left or right, there was no place to dodge. He could hear the creaking of the saddle leather right behind him.

"Don't shoot that hombre!" called a commanding voice, horribly close behind him. "Rope him, Mike! He's easy!"

Then a rifle cracked out of the brush at

the bending of the trail. The bullets whipped past the head of Derry. He glanced back and saw that no saddle behind him had been emptied, but that the men of the village were leaping their horses right and left to get out of the storm of lead.

Turning the corner at high speed, he saw Buck Rainey turning the black mare and putting his rifle back into its holster.

"That's the second time you've saved my hide!" shouted Tom Derry. "I won't forget!"

He saw Rainey wave a hand that banished the subject to a region of unimportance. Well, it was not unimportant to Tom Derry.

They were out of the ravine, now, taking a down grade that gave the wretched little mustang longer legs and a chance to get its wind. Derry could think, and it was only of one thing. Twice to owe his life, and to one man, was a staggering thing. He glanced across to the other and saw Rainey sitting the stride of the black mare magnificently, guiding the creature with the mere grip of his knees while his rapid hands refilled the magazine of his repeating rifle. And a passion came up in Derry to pay back the debt he owed to this man. If only the way

43

could be shown to him – if only the chance would come!

It came fast enough!

They were swinging, now, across a wide tableland, a high plateau that was pushed up among the mountains, and the hunt was regathering rapidly behind them.

"Go on by yourself!" shouted Derry. "You can get away, all right. Don't tie yourself down to me. I'll – I'll dodge them. Here, take the money – and that black mare will blow you away from them!"

He offered the sheaf of money. The wind got at it and rattled it loudly in his fingers.

"Keep it!" called Rainey. "Both or nothing, Tom. That's our motto!"

And this with the rifle bullets beginning to whistle once more through the air. But the miserable little bronco could not or would not improve its speed. And there was Rainey, keeping back his tall black within the range of trouble!

Then came the crash. The big black mare reared, leaped and then tried to bolt. She pulled away to a little distance before Derry saw the blood that streaked down her quarters. The animal had been hit and was bleeding fast. Their greatest source of strength had become weakness now.

Disaster followed before he could take breath. Rainey jerked aside in his saddle; when Derry pulled up to him, his whole right leg was being soaked with blood. He had been shot through the thigh, and it looked as though the bullet had nipped an artery.

"Go on," called Rainey. "They've stung me, and I've got to turn and fight them. Go on – for Barry Christian – understand? Go on to the Carys'. I'll stay here and cover you so – "

"Damn the running!" shouted Derry. "Both of us or neither of us. Make for the rocks there!"

A nest of rocks crowned a low hill on the left. Rainey, nodding, swung the black mare straight for it and let her sprint on a loosened rein, while he whipped out his rifle and opened fire on the pursuit. In spite of the fact that the black mare was galloping hard and jouncing her rider, the bullets of Rainey flew close enough to the mark to make the other riders scatter to either side. Two or three of them pulled up short and threw themselves down on the ground to reply to that running fire from a secure rest.

Before they could shoot, the two

fugitives were among the rocks, big Rainey slewing around out of the saddle and sinking to the ground. It was not in Derry's mind to remain there, however. He simply whipped out of his saddle and into Rainey's.

"Take the bronc. Ride on out of the way after I've pulled the gang off the trail. I'll come back – "

He flung those words over his shoulder as he started the wounded mare into frantic speed once more, and he heard Rainey shouting:

"Come back here! Don't be a fool! The mare's bleeding to death! Come back! They'll run you down!"

Well, that was all right. Already Rainey had twice saved his life, and a glory of hot pleasure came over Derry as he sprinted the black mare away from the rocks and across the plateau.

His ruse worked well enough. The pursuit had not closed in very far and in the slant dazzle of the late afternoon sun, they were recognizing a horse, not a rider. Just as Derry had hoped, every one of those riders swung away after the black mare.

They had to make a detour, at that, for the rifleman in the rocks had opened fire to

46

assist his partner, and the enemy was forced to swing away on a long slant before they could straighten out after the mare.

The black, poor thing, was in pain and fear enough to distend her nostrils and madden her eyes, but still she put all her heart into her work. The mare was a splendid mount, with a mouth of silk and the gait of flowing water. If she ran so well, she could surely jump a little, also.

And that might be important, for the whole face of the plateau, here, was criss-crossed by shallow little ravines that had been cut down by rivulets that ran only in the season of the rains. It was like a miniature of a complete river system, the water courses deeply incised. Derry tried the mare at a twelve-foot ditch of that sort. The black few it without trouble!

And suddenly Derry shouted with delight, for he could see the golden chance before him. All of those little ravines, of course, flowed along in one general direction, and in that direction he and Rainey had been fleeing. Now he turned his course and drove the mare right across the narrow of the valley. One little gulch after another opened up before him, and one after another the long-legged mare flew like a bird.

Derry looked back, and now he laughed out of a free and happy heart, for already the majority of the pursuers were struggling up and down across the little ravines. Only a single pair of riders could imitate the flying course of the black. Then, in turn, those leaders were gone. Like all the rest, they had to strain their horses up and down the steep sides of the gulches. It would take them half an hour to do what the mare could wing across in five minutes.

It seemed to take them even longer. In a mere breathing space they were dropped far behind. And a little later, Tom Derry had turned into a clump of woods and was working furiously over the bleeding wound of the mare. With water from a rivulet he washed the wound. With strips of the saddle blanket he bound in place a clean bandage of a newly laundered bandanna. And as the bleeding stopped, he sat down on a rock and eyed the mare, and saw her knees trembling with weakness or with fear, and watched the agony of fright go out of her big eyes. She came close to him. She would not graze more than a few yards from him. And when the wind came with a

48

rush through the trees, she snorted and limped quickly to his side.

Derry rubbed her nose, and looked at the sunset colours which were stretching around the horizon, seen by glimpses among the trunks of the trees. By this time, he judged, a disappointed set of riders had given up their man-hunt and were jogging down the home trail.

So he ventured out and led the lagging mare straight across country to the rocks. It was starlight when he reached them and found, of course, no sign of Rainey.

But even by scratching matches he was able to pick up a horse trail away from the rocks. It pointed toward a clump of trees a mere half mile from the rocks. But when he gained the grove and shouted, the voice of Rainey answered at once.

Derry halted, for the pleasure that he felt ran through his mind as a sweet taste runs through the tongue and the palate. A moment later he was in a little clearing among the trees and found there a bit of a fire, and Rainey calmly toasting bacon over the blaze!

"You're a cool devil, you are!" Derry said.

"No," answered Rainey. "The thick of

the trees is enough to keep this fire from being seen from outside the wood. My leg's too bad for any more riding, for a few days. They might as well catch me here as anywhere. And why not surrender with a full stomach instead of an empty one?"

Derry pointed to the rifle and the two revolvers that were laid out on the grass.

"There wouldn't have been any surrendering," he suggested.

"Oh, I don't know," answered Rainey. "How far did the boys follow you after you started the mare jumping the gulches? And how did you know she was a jumper?"

"She had the lift in her gallop," said Derry, "so I tried her, and found she could walk on air. Those fellows? Oh, they gave up pretty soon. What's the name of this mare?"

"Nell," said Rainey.

"Well," said Derry, "she's as game as anything that ever talked with a tongue."

"She simply does her bit," said Rainey calmly. It was as though he were speaking lightly of virtues found in his own family circle. "Sit down and eat. You can hear the water running, over there. Fill the pot for coffee, will you?"

"Before I take a look at the hole that's

drilled through your leg?" asked Derry.

"That? Oh, that's all right. I've dressed it as well as a doctor could. And if the germs stay out and the blood stays in, I'll be riding again in a week. It's only through the flesh."

Derry went down to the creek and filled the pot with water. As he came back, he was walking slowly, for it seemed to him that he had entered a new life – that everything he had done before that had been as nothing, and that he never before had found a real man – not even that hardy Yankee skipper, so handy with fists and tongue.

As he reached the fire, he suddenly extended his hand. Rainey took it with an almost hesitant gesture and, looking up, smiled into the face of Derry. And Rainey had the look, at that moment, of a very happy but rather guilty boy.

6

Cary Valley

Derry slept five hours on the flat of his back, as a sailor or a cowpuncher knows how to do. Then he wakened, saddled his mustang, patted the neck of Nell in farewell, and shook hands with Rainey. He parted quickly from the camp and took the way which Rainey had pointed out toward Cary Valley. There were still hours of darkness before him. He climbed with the horse through lonely valleys where the water sang loud or soft or came at him with rushings, like the wind. It seemed, sometimes, that if he turned aside to climb the slope of one of the mountains, he would be able to touch the stars when he gained the peak.

Those mountains were turning black, and the grey of the morning had commenced when he reached the wall of Cary Valley. As Rainey had suggested, he did not try to enter the valley by means of one of the gorges that pierced the wall of cliffs, for in the throat of such a valley he was fairly sure to encounter one of the clan, curious as children and cruel as Indians. Instead, he tethered his horse among trees near a place where he could descend the wall of cliffs, but on the edge of the rock he waited for a time while the light of the morning increased.

A land mist rose off the level like steam, as the dawn commenced. Through it, the clumps of the trees rose as dark islands. Finally, he could see the house itself, in the midst of the largest of those islands of woods. Then, the mist thinning out, the sparkle of creeks began to glimmer up to him. Last of all, he could see the grazing herds, spotted singly or in groups over that rich grazing land.

It was a special domain, he could see. The rough of the mountains had been mysteriously smoothed out here, and a private park established. Perhaps a glacier in another age had ploughed the surface flat inside that circle of cliffs.

He descended the cliff. In a crevice of the rocks, he thrust his wallet with the money of the bribe inside it. Then he went on across the level ground toward the Cary

53

house. He was walking in tall grass. There was plenty enough forage here to accommodate ten times the number of cattle that "Old Man" Cary grazed. But Rainey had explained that beforehand. Old Man Cary refused to make provisions of shelter and food to carry the stock through the bitter winters that occasionally struck the herd, and, therefore, it was decimated from time to time. Perhaps, said Rainey, it was the will of the old savage to keep his sons and grandsons from becoming soft with wealth. Money sounds many entrancing horns, and they all blow from distant horizons. Five years of wealth would probably disperse the tribe that still grew and held together in poverty.

By the time Derry came near the grove in which the house of Cary stood, smoke was rising from the many chimneys of it, and he heard the banging noises of doors closing, and the shrill babble of children. Dogs began to bark, and those rising sounds of life depressed him. They spoke too clearly of overwhelming numbers, and like most fighting men, Tom Derry was always seeing every question answered by an appeal to arms.

He came out now into the central

clearing that surrounded a long house. Rather, it was a succession of many log cabins, each shouldering against the other and making a line like one side of the street in a little English village, where one house helps to support its neighbour.

He had hardly appeared, when a number of big, wolfish dogs ran up to him, some howling, some growling. He knew enough to keep on walking steadily. If he paused, he had a feeling that the brutes would put their teeth into him without any further ado.

Then a swarm of children came at him, whooping. Not one of them had more than a single garment, half covering its body. They were as brown as Mexicans. They had long, black hair, and eyes of a sparkling black, too. They were beautiful children, he thought, but there was something that promised grossness in all their faces.

That swarm of youngsters set up a yelling that brought three men into doorways. When they spotted a stranger, each picked up a rifle that seemed to be at hand at every door, leaning against the wall, and they stepped out with the weapons.

Derry kept right on walking until a man

whose face was one great shag of black beard called out to him to stand. Then he halted. The fellow of the black beard approached him slowly from the front. The other two closed in on him from the sides.

"Who are you?" asked the bearded man.

Derry paused a moment before answering, because every tradition of Western hospitality was being blasted by this reception.

"Tom Derry is my name," he answered. "I want to see the old man."

"You *want* to see the old man?" asked the bearded fellow in surprise.

"Yes."

"Does the old man want to see you?"

"He'll be glad to see me after I've had a chance to talk to him for a time."

"Fan him, Dick," said the bearded Cary.

The other two stepped in close. Each took Tom Derry by an arm, and they searched him thoroughly.

He could be glad, now, that he had not brought the money with him. It would have been seized before it had accomplished any purpose whatever. They got the gun which Rainey had given him, and his big jack-knife. Those were his only weapons and they were all that interested the Carys.

"Ask the old man if he wants to see this hombre," said the bearded man, and the fellow called Dick disappeared into the house.

Others of the tribe were appearing now. Women stood with their arms akimbo in the doorways – big women with flashing eyes. Men lounged at the entrances, pretending to take small heed of the stranger. And the little tide of children kept right up around Tom Derry.

Dick now reappeared, and with him there was a slender girl, bare-footed, bare-legged, with the white of a recent thorn scratch over one calf. She was both slender and round. She might have been anything from fifteen to eighteen. The flash of her black eyes ignited something in the heart of Tom Derry.

She came up close to him and stood with one hand on her hip, staring right into his eyes.

"Who are you?" she asked.

"Tom Derry."

"That's just a name," said the girl. "What do you want?"

"A chance to talk to the old man."

"The old man sent me out to find what you are."

57

"I'm an ordinary hombre," said Derry, "with two feet and two hands, and all that."

"Two pretty good hands, I'm thinking," said the girl.

"What makes you think that?"

"You didn't smash that knuckle on a stone, I guess."

He looked down at the flattened knuckle and remembered the day he had swung his weight behind that hand and against the jaw of a certain wide-faced German in a forecastle brawl.

"Anyway," said Derry, "I'm not going to talk to the old man with my hands."

The girl kept staring into his eyes, as though his words meant very little compared with the meaning she got out of his looks.

"Well," she said at last, "he's on a grouch this morning, but if you want to chance him, come ahead. Bring him in, boys."

She walked ahead of them, and Tom Derry watched the rhythm that played through her from the light-stepping feet to the toss of her head. She was as bold and free as a man, but there were unknown treasures of femininity in her. He felt a queer, giddy lifting of the heart as he wondered what man would be able to stir her.

He was taken into a cabin as poverty-stricken as anything he had ever seen. The logs had not been hewn flat on the inner surfaces. The floor was beaten earth, and not very well beaten down, at that. All the furniture he saw – there was little of it – was axe-and-knife made, a home product. He saw, as he passed through the rooms, ponderous tables of split logs laid over sawbucks, a few chairs with straight backs, but chiefly stools and benches. He saw some Indian beds of willow slats rolled up in corners, the bedding piled in ugly heaps on top. The stale smell of the sleepers was still in the air, and other odours, of cookery, could not waken his appetite.

In this way Derry was brought into a small back room where a bit of a fire wavered under a big black pot that hung from a crane over the hearth. Near the hearth sat a man so old that his face had shrunk to boyish dimensions. It was oddly unmatched compared with his big dome of a skull. He wore, like an Indian, trousers and moccasins only, and Tom Derry saw how time had parched that great body, leaving only parchment skin, and the pull of great tendons showing through the meagreness of dried-up muscles. Once he must have been a giant, but now his strength was limited to the cleaning of guns, perhaps – a whole rack of them was near him – or his present labour of sharpening knives. He had an oilstone on his knee, and he worked a great bowie knife over the whetstone, keeping the blade instinctively at the perfect bevel.

He said, without looking up: "What you find out, M'ria?"

"I found a man," said Maria.

"Think you'd find a dog, maybe?" asked the old man.

"Sometimes I do," said Maria. "Here he is, Grandpa."

The grandfather looked slowly up. His eyes were almost veiled by the excessively drooping folds of the eyelids, but the spark of life was bright and active under those hollow brows.

He stared at Tom Derry. Like utter barbarians, none of these people were contented by glances, but had to bear down with full weight on whatever they regarded.

"His name's Tom Derry," said the girl. "He's been around a lot. He's a good man with his hands. He had sense enough to come into the valley without taking one of the creeks to show him the way. He wants to talk to you."

This brief summing up was so to the point that Tom Derry felt more than a bit uneasy. If the girl were a type of the clan, then the grown men would be able to see through him like a plate of glass.

The old man said: "Come over here."

Derry stepped closer, and halted for the inspection.

"Yeah, you been around," said the old man, nodding. "It's gettin' so that I can trust M'ria's eyes to see a few little things. Wait a minute. What makes you think he's been around such a lot, M'ria?"

"There's a queer knot in that hat cord," said the girl. "It would take a sailor to tie that knot. And he walks loose in the knees, like a sailor."

"Yeah, you got a pair of eyes, and some sense behind 'em. Stranger, how'd you want to talk to me?"

"Alone," said Derry.

"Clear 'em out," said the old man. "I'm goin' to have trouble with this hombre, but he can start it his own way!"

7

The Bargain

It was to Tom Derry as though he were in an alien land, in a fortress, where the armed men were capable of treating him like a spy. The old man regarded him for a moment after the room was cleared of the others, except the girl.

"I'd better talk to you alone," said Derry, nodding toward Maria.

"Leave her here," said the old man. "She's all right. She can keep her jaws locked over little things, and big things she wouldn't understand, anyway."

The girl laughed.

"Shut up your laughin'," said the old man. "Look at that soup and give it a stir, and shut up your laughin'. It's time for me to have something to eat."

She said: "The soup's all right, but it's not time for you to have it."

"I'll have what I want when I want it," said he.

"You'll have what's good for you," answered Maria.

"You brat!" he cried in his husky, bubbling voice. "Are you goin' to try to set yourself again' me?"

"D'you think it's any fun for me to take care of you and your temper?" asked the girl.

"M'ria!" cried the old man, angrily, sorrowfully.

"Be quiet," said Maria. "I'm not going to leave you, but sometimes I'm half minded to. Ask him what he wants."

"What did you say your name is?" asked the old man.

"Tom Derry."

"Tom Derry, you been a sailor. What are you doin' this far into dry land?"

"I'm bringing some good news to you."

"Yeah? Good news never comes before sun-up. Speak out and lemme see what you got in your head."

"Money," said Derry.

"How much?"

"Enough for you and your tribe," said Derry.

"I kind of like to hear you talk. You talk like you had sense. Maybe you have. So tell me how we're goin' to make money."

63

"By cracking the jail in Blue Water."

"Yeah, that jail could be cracked. Not that we'd do it. We're law-abidin' people, Derry."

"Sure you are," said Derry. "You abide by the law if you can find it. But law is a long way off, up here in the Blue Waters."

The old man chuckled.

"Some friend of yours in the jail?"

"I never saw him. I'm only the messenger. His name is Barry Christian. Do you know him?"

The old man leaned back in his chair.

"M'ria," he said, "gimme a drink of corn liquor and then call the boys and tell 'em to see how far they can throw this hombre out of the valley. I don't care if he lands on a hard spot, neither."

The girl picked up a heavy earthenware jug that might have held five gallons or more. She handled it easily, and poured some into a tin cup. She tasted it, taking a good swallow, and the fire of the stuff could not take the thoughtful look out of her eyes. She gave what was left in the cup to the old man. She poured some more into another tin. It was not a cup but a cooking tin. This she proffered to Derry.

He took it, very much surprised. The

liquid was not colourless. It had a faint stain of yellow in it. It was very pungent, but went down pleasantly.

"Hey!" yelled the old man. "I didn't tell you to give him a drink. I told you to throw him out of the house. I told you to call the boys and throw him out."

"Let him talk. He ain't poisoned you just by naming a name, has he?" said the girl.

The old man glowered at her. Then he kicked a gong that was beside his chair. It brought a rush of footfalls. Two doors were thrown open, and the armed men began to pour into the room.

"Take M'ria!" shouted the old man. "I'm goin' to teach her. Take M'ria and take the stranger, and throw 'em both – "

He choked and coughed. Big, capable hands seized on Tom Derry and the girl.

She said to one of the ruffians who had gripped her: "Stop smashing my bones, Joe. I'll make you wish your hands had rotted off before you laid 'em on me!"

"I'm goin' to teach the brat what I can do in Cary Valley!" roared the old man. "I'm goin' to show her!"

"Yeah. We'll do what you say," said the man of the black beard.

The old man hesitated.

65

"Go on!" cried Maria fiercely. "Don't dodder like an old fool. Tell them what to do with us."

"You hear what she called me?" shouted the old man, heaving himself up from his chair.

But when he reached his feet, he wavered a little. He was immensely old. Surely he had seen a hundred years if he had seen a day.

"Maybe I've given her lesson enough. Leave her be. Get out of here!" he said to the men.

"Yeah, and what about the stranger?" asked one of the men.

"Grandpa hasn't finished talking to him," said the girl.

The old man glared at her, opened his lips to shout another command, and then wound up weakly with:

"You boys get out and stay where I can call you. I may be needin' you soon, and not for no false alarm."

The Carys trooped out of the room and slammed the doors. Their muttering voices receded.

"Smoke your pipe, Grandpa," said the girl. "That soothes you down a good deal when you get all on edge this way."

He had settled back in the chair and reached for a pipe and a pouch filled with shredded tobacco.

"You try to make a fool out of me!" he declared to Maria.

"I try to keep you from making a fool out of yourself," said the girl. "Ease off your high horse and be comfortable. Nobody's trying to steal your shoes."

"Christian! That crook comes and tries to talk to me about Barry Christian!" said the old man.

The girl held a light for the pipe; the old man began to smack his lips as he pulled on it. Presently he was squinting through a cloud of smoke. There was a big twist of dirty string around the stem of the pipe to keep it more easily inside his gums. From the uncertain, loose corners of his mouth, a dribble worked out, now and then, and the girl, with a quick hand and not much reverence in her touch, wiped his chin dry.

"The whisky'll work on you pretty soon, and then you'll feel a lot better," she said.

"Don't tell me how I'll feel," said the old man. "I've had enough of your lip. One of these here days you're goin' to get me real mad, and I'm goin' to put my foot down. You give a hand and a drink to this gent that comes up here talkin' about Christian, do you?"

"Why not?" asked Maria. "He can name the devil if he wants to, can't he? I've heard you do it, and put him in hell, too."

"Nobody can name Barry Christian up here," said the old man. "The skunk that got us into trouble with Jim Silver and turned everybody agin' us. Except that folks now know that we hate Christian, I dunno what they'd likely do to us."

"It would take a whole lot of folks to bother you up here in this valley," suggested Derry.

"He's getting old and scary," remarked Maria.

"Who? What?" shouted the old man. "I'll slap your face for you, you young rat!"

"Be honest, Grandpa," she persisted. "You're scared about everything that may happen."

He puffed at his pipe, choked with fury and smoke.

"It's got so people can't even talk to you," Maria went on. "Pretty soon, you'll be babbling to yourself all day long, making no sense, just like a baby that's crawling around. Here's a man who's never seen Christian, but he's got money to pay you to help Christian. Ain't messengers got a right to a good reception, no matter how you damn the gents that send them?"

"I got half of a mind," said the old man, "to have you hosswhipped, M'ria, right up close where I could hear you holler. You wouldn't be the first gal in this valley that's had to eat the whip. But doggone me, if you don't spit fire and sense mixed in together. Lemme hear what this hombre has to say."

The girl turned to Derry with an eloquent gesture, as much as to point out that she had opened the way for him, and that at least he could speak to the point.

He said: "You fellows have a good set, in Blue Water. People think you hate Christian. The whole gang of you could get right up close to the jail and nobody would ever suspect you. Isn't that right?"

"Mostly that's right."

"They take Barry Christian out to hang him, tomorrow."

"That's what I hear."

"They'll hang him right up to a tree, I've heard. They want people to see the execution. They want to set an example by it. Is that right?"

"A good thing for the world, when Barry Christian chokes on a rope," said the old man.

"That may be. But what should keep you and the rest of the Cary men from being in that crowd and making a rush at the right time?"

"Nothin' could keep us, much, except that we'd be strung up later on, one by one," said the old man.

"Who would string you up?" asked Derry.

"There's maybe more folks in the world than you think on," said the old man.

"It takes hard men to ride this far and get over the wall into this place. And the law doesn't care. It's too high in the mountains for the law to care. You're above the law here."

The old man actually smiled.

"Young feller," he said, "*you* rode up here and got in. Are you a hard man?"

"Try me," said Tom Derry, grinning in turn.

"Ay," said the old man. "Fists has changed your face. Fists and other things. Maybe there's a right tidy bit of man in him, M'ria."

"Maybe he's so-so," said the girl, eyeing Derry with perfect calm. "His weight's in the right place."

"We're wastin' time though," said the old man. "You can't hire this gang to lift a hand for Barry Christian."

"I've got a price to offer you," went on Derry. "Name a price for the job yourself."

"There ain't any money that would hire me to send my family into that job. Not for fifty thousand dollars."

"How about ten thousand spot cash?" asked Derry.

"I told you he meant something," said Maria, confidently nodding. "He's not here just to talk and blow. Money is better than a kick in the face."

"Ten thousand? I wouldn't budge the boys for ten thousand," said the grandfather. "Besides, I ain't goin' to budge 'em, anyway, for Barry Christian."

"I could get the job done cheaper," declared Derry. "I could buy up plenty of men right down there in Blue Water – men that aren't so afraid of the law. But the thing might get noised around before the deal went through. That's the only reason I'm up here, and I'll make you a flat, and final, offer of fifteen thousand dollars."

"I wouldn't budge for thirty thousand," said the old man, with determination.

"Why not talk business instead of

making jokes?" asked Derry.

"I don't want to talk business. I've got enough to keep me busy now."

The old man resumed his work on the sharpening of the bowie knife.

"All right," said Derry. "I've done my best and offered you my limit. So long."

"So long," said the old man. "I'm glad to see your back."

"Wait a minute, Grandpa," put in the girl. "You wanta think it over a bit. Turn twenty thousand dollars into horseflesh, and saddles, and gunpowder, and guns. Then what d'you think?"

"I didn't offer twenty thousand," said Derry.

"You will, though," said the girl. "You've got a good heart and you'll peg the bet up a little. Twenty thousand is a lot of money."

"Twenty-five thousand is a lot more," answered the old man.

"Sure it is. And a million is better still," said Derry carelessly, determined that they should not extract the ultimate penny from him.

"Twenty-five thousand is a good round sum," said Cary. "A man could out and do something for twenty-five thousand. It sounds like something and it *is* something."

"What makes you think that anybody's scalp is worth twenty-five thousand?" asked Derry.

"Some is worth more. Some a lot more. There's Jim Silver. Ain't Christian spent fortunes and fortunes tryin' to get the throat of Silver cut? Twenty-five thousand is cheap to get a man saved by folks that hate his innards."

"Anything might be cheap, if a man had it," said Derry. "You might as well ask me for fifty thousand."

"Don't stand around in my light, then," answered Cary. "Get out of here and stop botherin' me."

Tom Derry answered hotly: "You people that want the world with a fence around it – you make me sick. Good-bye! I'll take my money where people have brains enough to know what it's worth."

"Go along with you," said Maria. "You'll be back again."

He turned on her with a rather childish fury.

"What makes you think that I've got twenty-five thousand?" he demanded.

"By the way it hit you in the eye when Grandpa named the price. I could see you read the dollar sign and the figures after it."

"The whole Cary tribe isn't worth that much money," Derry said fiercely.

"Say that to a Cary man, and he'll show you some new ways of tying knots," said Maria. "He'll tie them in you."

"Shut up and get out!" commanded the old man.

"I'll get out," said Derry. "Twenty-five thousand? I laugh at you! I could buy your whole valley for half the price."

"Grandpa would throw in some boot," said Maria.

"What sort of boot?" asked the old man.

"Me, for instance," said Maria. "The stranger likes me pretty well. Don't you, Tom?"

"He's got more sense than to look at a spindlin', long-legged heifer with no meat on the bones, like you," said the old man. "What makes you set your cap for this mug of a Tom Derry, anyway, M'ria?"

"Oh, I dunno," said the girl. "It's just by way of bargaining."

Tom Derry was still staring at her. He could not speak for a time. Then he said:

"Well, I'll pay twenty-five thousand."

"All right, all right," said the old man.

74

"Shut up the yappin' and get the money, then."

"How would I know that you'll go through with the deal after I give you the cash?"

"You'll take my word for it," said Old Man Cary.

Derry smiled. "I thought we were talking business," he suggested.

"All right, go fetch me a Bible, M'ria," said the old man, "and I'll swear on it like a regular lawyer."

"That's no good," the girl told Derry. "Make him shake hands on it, and he'll never quit the bargain."

"Shut your fool face!" shouted Old Man Cary.

"Here's my hand," offered Derry, grinning.

"I hope it rots!" cried the old man. "M'ria, you throwin' in with strangers agin' your own kind?"

"He's paying the price, and I'm thrown in for boot," said Maria carelessly.

"Twenty-five thousand it is," said Derry.

The old man reached up tentatively, then, with a sudden and surprising grip, he took the hand of Derry.

"It's done!" he said, "and the more fool I am. If I loose M'ria, I gotta break another half-witted gal to my ways."

8

Speeding Trouble

The old man kicked the gong once more. There was the same instant appearance of the armed clansmen. To them the grandfather said: "Take and treat this gent well. Leave your guns be still. Where he wants to go, leave him go. Where he wants to come, leave him come. He's had my hand, and I've had his hand. Now, all of you clear out. Tom Derry, bring me that money."

Derry went out from the house. As he stood in the open, he saw the girl beside him. Her face was perfectly calm, but her eyes were bright and uneasy.

"How old are you, Maria?" he asked.

"I'm twenty," said the girl.

"You're nearer to fourteen," he told her.

"I was seventeen last week," she said.

"You'd start right off with lying?" he asked her.

"Of course I would," answered Maria. "I mean, until a man marries me, why should I tell the truth? It's all bargaining. How old are you?"

"Me? I'm only twenty-seven."

"Minus five," said Maria.

"All right," Tom Derry grinned. "Twenty-two is easy to write and easy to remember. Will you listen to me?"

"Yes, if it don't take too long."

"Get a pair of horses, and we can talk while I go for the money."

"I'll get 'em. Come along."

She took him to a big corral behind the house, and brought out a pair of ropes. One she gave him. The other she took herself.

"Snag the cayuse you want for yourself," said the girl, and vaulted over the fence with the ease of a man.

He was fairly good with a rope, but these mustangs fled like quicksilver before Derry. When he cornered the group that contained the fine grey he wanted, the whole lot turned and charged at him like so many devils. As they went by, he saw through the whirling dust clouds that the rope of the girl was already on the neck of an active little roan. She saddled her horse and sat on the top rail of the fence.

She wore overalls of a faded blue. They were much too big for her and had evidently been handed down by one of the Cary men. She patched them with half a dozen fragments of different colours across the knees and the seat. She had battered old moccasins on her feet, and she wore a shirt of checked flannel. She wore no hat. In the house her hair was down her back; now it was twisted about her head. She sat there with her legs crossed, smoking a cigarette, watching. She looked more like an Indian than ever, immobile, full of thoughts which Tom Derry could not fathom.

He tried and tried the wicked little devil of a grey, over and over again. Dust blinded him. Sweat stung his eyes. He finally nailed the dodging ghost more by luck than by skill and brought it out of the corral and saddled it. The girl said nothing. She simply kept smoking and watching.

Such anger grew up in him as he had never known before. It was fury, but there was an ache in his heart, also. He said to the girl:

"You ought not to smoke, Maria."

"No?" said the girl.

And she blew a long, slow breath of smoke full in his face.

"You took a drink in there, too," said he. "You want to quit booze and

79

smoking."

"Yeah?" said the girl, and blew more smoke in his face.

He took the cigarette out of her hand and threw it into the dust. She struck him with the flat of her hand. It moved faster than the jerk of a cat's paw. The weight of the blow knocked the hat off his head; the sting of it brought tears into his eyes, and out of the distance he heard a loud, bawling chorus of male laughter, and the squealing delight of children.

He picked up the hat and resettled it on his head. The laughter continued from the house. Maria was twisting up another cigarette, her fingers seeing their own way about the business, while she gave her eyes to a calm survey of him. With half-dreamy amusement she smiled at him. Then, taking a pack of matches out of a pocket of her shirt, she scratched one and lighted the smoke. He picked the cigarette from between her lips.

There was the same flash of her hand. He tried to parry it, but it was inescapably swift. As well try to ward the thrust of a snake's head. The hard fingers whipped home across in his mouth; bruising his lips. There was a taste of blood in his mouth; the

80

yelling laughter grew louder still. But suddenly he smiled at the girl.

"All right," he said. "Get on your horse."

She slipped from the fence. He mounted; the grey started to pitch, but the first grip of Derry's long, iron-hard legs told the mustang that bucking would be a poor amusement this day. It relaxed to a dog-trot, and he rode straight off from the corral, heading away among the trees. Behind him, he was aware that the laughter had stopped. The blood was roaring in his ears like a waterfall. Or was it the noise of a wind pouring through the branches of the trees?

He came out into the open, with the brightness of the grassy plain spread out before him in the softest of undulations. As he jogged on, he was aware that another horse was cantering behind him. One of Cary men, perhaps, had followed to plague him. Then the head of a roan horse worked up beside the grey. Out of the tail of his eye he could see the girl and her smile.

A harder beat of hoofs rushed at him. He turned his head not a whit, but he knew that trouble was speeding toward him on the back of that third mustang.

81

9

The Ride

As that unseen rider came up, something shot out from his hand. Like the force of a watching eye, Derry felt the danger and doubled over in his saddle. The noose of a rope slithered over his shoulder.

He caught it out of the air and, giving it a half-hitch around the horn of his saddle, he made his mustang sit down against the coming jerk. The pony braced itself like a good cattle horse, and across the eyes of Derry raced a young man with the shoulders of an Atlas. The Cary youth was pulling vainly at the rope as he went by on a black horse. Then the lariat snapped taut, the strain taking the black horse from a sidelong angle, and it was jerked flat on the ground. The rider sailed on into the air, landed in a somersault, came staggering to his feet.

He had a knife in his belt and a revolver in a holster worn well down his thigh. If he started using weapons, he would cross Derry off the map, and Derry knew it. So he hit the ground almost as soon as the Cary youth. He went in with a headlong rush.

He had been right. The Colt that the fellow drew looked to Tom Derry as long as a rifle, and it flashed like a sword in his eyes. With all the weight of his charge behind the blow, Derry hammered a long, overhand punch on the very button of the jaw. The Cary youth did not fall backwards. He wavered, and then slumped on his face.

Tom Derry took the black horse, because it was bigger and better than the grey. He recoiled the rope on the pommel of the saddle as he cantered forward again. Behind him, he knew that the fallen man was rising. He knew that the girl was coming, also, on her roan. He wondered, with a cold shuddering in his spinal marrow, if a bullet was about to crash into him. But he rode on without turning his head.

And no gun sounded behind him!

Presently the girl came up beside him. He would not look squarely at her, but he could see that she was smiling at distance in perfect content.

They paused on the bank of a shallow creek, half crystal and half white riffle. They would have to cross that. But as they sat their horses side by side, Derry reached over and pulled from the pocket of the checked shirt her sack of tobacco and the wheat-straw papers. He stowed them in his own pocket, and then rode down to the edge of the water. He let the black have a swallow or two of the pure stream. They waded on across. The water came up almost to the stirrups; the force of the current made the horses slip and stagger. He saw the girl lean to dip a handkerchief in the water.

When they had climbed the farther slope, she said: "There's blood on your face, Tom."

He knew it was there.

"It's the blood you drew. No Cary man drew it," he said.

"Wait a minute," said Maria. With the wet handkerchief she rubbed away the dried blood carefully. "Your mouth's a little swollen. I'm sorry, Tom."

But she kept smiling. She was not sorry. He was baffled by the odd mixture of submission and wolfish revolt in her.

They rode on toward the wall of the

valley, where he had left the money.

All the time his heart was lifting, giddily. The sky was bluer than he had ever seen it. The clouds were a most dazzling white. He wanted to laugh aloud and look frankly at the girl, but every time he glanced at her, he saw the curiously brooding smile that he could not decipher.

"Maria," he said, "I don't like your name."

She said nothing. She simply turned her half-smile on him and waited.

"I'm calling you Mary from now on," said Derry. "I like Molly better still. Make a choice between them."

"Molly," said the girl.

More than ever he wanted to laugh. He had to keep his teeth gripped hard together. A hawk slid on wide, transparent wings out of a treetop close beside them. He snatched out his revolver and fired. The big bird dodged away at redoubled speed. Another gun spoke from the hand of Molly, and the hawk shot down to earth and landed with a thud.

The girl rode up to it. At a canter she passed the spot, leaned swiftly from the saddle, and brought up the dead bird by the legs. Its wings fanned out as in life as

85

she cut back to the cantering black mustang. She offered the prize to Derry.

"I don't want it," he told her.

"Didn't you have no want for it? Just foolishness?" she asked him.

"You watch your way of speaking," said Tom Derry. "You talk like a half-breed that's never been in school."

"All right," she said.

"When I come back for you, one of these days, I hope you'll be talking as straight as a book."

"All right."

He frowned at her, and she began to laugh. The laughter went out.

"You're not taking me away with you?" she asked. "Not when you go?"

"No. I'm coming back for you, one day. Will you be here?"

She said nothing. Somehow, he felt that it would be both foolish and dangerous to repeat the question. She was as moody as spring weather, as changeable, and there was always danger in her.

When they got to the wall of the valley, he found the crevice and the wallet in it. As he lifted the money and pocketed it, he saw the girl watching him with savage eyes.

"I dunno," she said. "I might up and fill

you full of lead and take all that kale and be rich. Why shouldn't I do it?"

"Because you're just a fool girl," said Derry. "That's the only reason you don't do it."

"I've chucked myself at your head, and you don't give a rap for me," she said.

"How many times have you chucked yourself at a man?" he asked.

"Only once before. There was a big hombre up here named Clonmel. He was the biggest thing I ever saw. He'd make two of you. He had looks, too. I tried to chuck myself at him, but his head was all full of a gal called Julie and there wasn't room in his eyes to see a mug like me."

"You're not a mug. You're a fine-looking girl," said Derry. "This Clonmel was a dummy."

"You'd never say that to his face."

"I'd say it to his face any day," declared Derry.

"Would you? He could throw the Carys around like nothing, so what would he do to you?"

"The Carys are not so tough," said Derry.

"No? You're one of the few tough ones, eh?"

"I don't say that. I aim to get along without trouble."

"Nope. You pride yourself on being hard. You're hard enough to be a partner of Barry Christian. That's how tough you are."

"Christian isn't tough," said Derry.

"No, poison isn't tough," she answered.

"He's just a man that isn't understood," said Derry.

"Say, what are you trying to give me?" asked Maria Cary. "Are you trying to talk to me about Barry Christian?"

"He's one of the finest men in the world!" said Derry hotly.

"Sure he is," said the girl. "A razor is one of the finest things in the world, too – for cutting throats."

She laughed.

"You must think I'm a half-wit," she told Derry.

He mounted, and she rode beside him on the home trail. He said no more about Barry Christian, because he was too deeply angered. In a deep silence they cantered the horses through the watery swishing of the grass until they came close to the house. Then half a dozen riders appeared out of the trees and charged in a body, yelling like

Indians. Derry pulled up the black to a quick halt.

"Come on!" shouted the girl to him. "Don't show yellow or they'll eat you. It's only a bluff to see if you're a real man. Don't make a fool of yourself and of me!"

She was very angry. She was tense and stiff with passion, staring back at him. So he sent the black ahead at a gallop. He saw Molly pull wide of him, to leave him alone to handle the charge; and now, with a rush, the Carys were at him. Ropes swung in the air; voices thundered; the flash of their eyes was like the glitter of naked guns; their horses were stretched out level with their speed.

Well, resistance was out of the question, and Derry lifted his head and kept his face calm as he rode through the cyclone. It raged around him; it was gone to a distance; and the yelling turned into tumultuous laughter. Then the girl pulled back to his side as they entered the shade of the trees.

"Clonmel would have known how to handle them," she said curtly.

"The devil with Clonmel!" said Derry. "Why do you throw him in my face?"

"He's a standard for measuring men,"

she answered, "and it's by him that I find you short."

Their eyes flared at one another almost with hate; but he thought she was prettier then than ever.

They reached the house, dismounted, and half a dozen of the tall Cary women paused in front of the rambling cabin with huge baskets of soiled laundry poised on their heads. They were going down to the creek to do the day's washing. They halted a moment to stare like handsome wild animals at the stranger.

Past them, Derry entered the house with the girl leading the way, stepping fast, never looking back at him. She brought him straight into the room of the old man, where the air was stale and humid with the steam of the soup.

There they found a strapping girl of twenty to whom the old man was saying:

"It ain't a hard job; it's an easy job. But you gotta keep your eyes open and move when I tell you to move. Maybe I'll have to damn you for a few days, but then you'll get the hang of the work and – "

He broke off to say: "Hello, M'ria. Back here so soon with your man?"

"He's no man of mine," she said. "He

ain't even a boy."

She marched up to the other girl, and anger seemed to swell in her body.

"Get out of here!" cried Maria. "Get out before I sail into you. You big numb-headed cow, take your hoofs out of here!"

"Grandpa called me in. He's sick of you – he doesn't want you back," answered the other girl stoutly.

"You lie!" said Maria furiously. "Did you dare to say you were sick of me, Grandpa?" she added to the old man.

The grandfather rubbed his knuckles over his chin. "I thought you'd gone and left me," he said, "and Bertha, there, might be a good gal to take your place. Would you come back and stay, M'ria?" he added wistfully.

"I'll stay as long as I can stand you!" answered Maria. "You – get out!"

She snatched from the wall the dangling lash of a black-snake, as she spoke, and slashed at Bertha with it. There was a scream of fear; Bertha vanished, and the old man lay contentedly back in his chair, laughing heartily.

"You kind of gimme an appetite," said the grandfather. "It's good to lay eyes on you, M'ria. Are you through with this here

Tom Derry?"

"I'm through with him."

"The more fool you," said the grandfather unexpectedly. "Here, lad. Where's the money?"

Tom Derry counted out the greenbacks rapidly. The stack amounted to exactly twenty-five thousand dollars. Old Man Cary folded it and shoved it in a great wad inside his belt, right against his bare, yellowish skin.

"All right," he said. "Tomorrow we'll be down there in Blue Water in time for the hangin'."

"There'll be no hanging. You fellows will do your job?" asked Derry doubtfully.

The old man gaped at him.

Then he said: "You tell him, M'ria."

She said, with scorn: "Grandpa shook hands with you, didn't he? That means that every man in the Cary Valley will die, if he has to, to put the deal through. Now get out. We're thoroughly tired of you, around here."

The old man began laughing huskily.

Said Tom Derry: "You've got teeth and claws, and I've seen them. But when I want you, I'll come back here and get you."

"You'll come and get me!" cried the girl.

"No, you stay with Barry Christian and his crooks. I don't want to see the face of you, ever again. Get out!"

She struck the floor with the lash of the whip and Tom Derry delayed only long enough to see that part of the brightness in her eyes was tears. Then he left.

10

At Blue Water

Barry Christian was not brought out to be hung the next day. He was given a reprieve of five days by the governor's authority, no one knew why. The real truth was that more news-hawks wanted to get to the spot to make pictures with their cameras and with their words of the last moments of the famous man.

That was why Tom Derry had a chance to get back to Buck Rainey and talk with him. Buck's leg was nearly healed, even in this short time. He could walk with not a very great limp. He explained that he would soon be riding, and in the meantime, he had all that he wished. He only desired that Barry Christian should be brought in that direction after the delivery.

To that Tom Derry assented. He merely remarked: "There seems to be a whole lot of people who think that Christian's a crook."

"Ay, you know how it is," said Rainey. "There are some men so big that we either have to hate them or envy them or fear them. We can't meet them on their own level and so we pretend that they've sold their souls to the devil."

Tom Derry nodded. He could not help remarking, however: "A lot of people seem to think that Jim Silver's the greatest man in the world."

"Sneaking hypocrites always have a big following," answered Buck Rainey. "Only the people who have seen the money change hands know the right men from the bought men."

He said this so heartily that Derry answered: "I'll leave it to you. You ought to know, Buck."

"Why leave it to me?" said Buck Rainey, with a little touch of sharpness. "I might be bamboozling you, as far as that goes. Find out the truth for yourself."

"I won't bother," replied Derry. "I trust you, Buck, and that's enough for me."

"Suppose that I were wrong?" asked Rainey.

Derry laughed a little at the thought.

"Then murder would be too sweet for you," he said finally. "A man who would fool a friend is the worst skunk in the world."

Rainey, however, did not laugh, but studied his friend for some time with his keen eyes. At length he turned the talk on the Carys and what had happened in the strange valley among the mountains. When Derry had answered, Buck asked:

"What about the girl?"

"Well, I've told you. There she is. There's nobody like her."

"You love her?"

"Love is a word I've read about," said Derry. "I wouldn't use it any too free. My mother was a great one. She used to make me go and cut the switches that she licked me with. But I loved her. I don't know anybody else. Perhaps this girl. I don't know."

"I mean, are you hungry to have her? Do you ache for her?"

"Ay. I ache, well enough. She almost run me out of the valley, but she sticks in behind my eyes and won't go away. She's better to look at than roast meat when you're starving. She can ride better than a man. She can shoot straighter than I can. She'd take the devil by his chin whiskers and wag his head for him. I never saw such a girl."

"What made her turn against you?" asked Rainey.

"She thought I was talking down to her. She thought I didn't mean what I said."

"She'll learn better than that."

Tom Derry shook his head. "I'll tell you," he said. "To get some girls is harder than to kill some men. They won't believe that they like you till you're nearly dead. I'll be near dead or dying, before she ever knows her own mind. Back in her head there's a fellow called Clonmel. Know about him?"

"I can tell you about him in three words – Jim Silver's brother."

"As bad as Silver?"

"The same blood in him."

A sudden great doubt made Derry exclaim: "Suppose that you were wrong!"

"Yes, you can suppose that," agreed the other. "Now, you'd better get back to Blue Water and fetch Christian out of jail. Work it with the sheriff and the Carys. As soon as the sheriff knows that you're a friend of the Carys, he'll make sure that you hate Christian. He'll even let you visit Barry in the jail. Then you can talk to him and tell him things."

"Say it over again," asked Derry. "Why do the Carys hate Christian so?"

"Because he got them into trouble with Silver, and Silver made them out a set of crooks, in the eyes of everyone. To be a Cary was a proud thing, in the old days. To be one now is like being a mountain lion or any wildcat that asks its belly what it should do next."

Derry took a long breath.

"I'd like to meet Jim Silver," he said slowly. "I'd give my heart to talk to him."

"You'll probably be dead before he speaks to you," answered Rainey.

But when Derry rode back to Blue Water, he was still in a strange degree of doubt. That question in the back of his mind had been answered only in part, and he had to ask it over and over again. He came on an old Mexican at a winding of the trail over Blue Water and he looked into the lack-lustre eyes of the ancient man for a moment before he said:

"Partner, what d'you know about Jim Silver?"

"If you are his friend, I salute you, señor. If you are his enemy, the good God forgive you!"

The Mexican went on his way, and poor

98

Derry, sorely troubled, continued into Blue Water.

On the edge of the town, in a cluster of leather tents that would have been appropriate for Indians in the old days, he found the clan of the Carys. There were twenty grown men and one boy, who was called "Chuck." There was one woman, and that was Maria, who had come to take care of the old man, who insisted on being present.

Derry, making for the tents, found a camp-fire burning and the Carys sitting about it on their heels or cross-legged, toasting meat on wooden splinters. Derry went in among them, found the meat, carved some chunks, and roasted his portion along with the others. Those wild men received him as though he had been an image out of thin air. They did not talk to him. They did not seem to see him.

Presently the girl came out and dipped a pannikin into the big iron pot in which coffee was seething. Derry stood up beside her.

"Where's the old man?" he asked.

"He's with Sheriff Walt Milton," she said. She looked away from him.

"I'll go in with you," said Derry.

99

When Derry ducked after her through the entrance flap, he saw the grim face of Walt Milton, and he saw the old man leaning against a back rest, with his legs stuck out straight before him. It was nearly sunset, and a dimly rosy light filled the tent. The two men looked at him for a moment. It seemed that the old man had forgotten him.

At last he said: "Walt, this here is Tom Derry. Friend of mine. Hates the heart of Christian. Wants to see him in the jail before he stretches his neck. Fix him up, will you? Tom, this is Walt Milton. He calls himself a sheriff."

Milton reached up a hand, and the pair shook hands. The girl was pouring out coffee for the two men.

"Drop around before nine in the morning," said the sheriff. "I'll fix you up so's you can damn Christian a few times. You ain't the only one."

He chuckled as he said this, and a sharp distaste formed like a sourness in the back of Derry's throat.

He went out of the tent and stood in the darkening of the day, trying to put two and two together, and disliking very much the part that lay before him. He would go to

100

the jail in the morning and try to form an attachment to Christian. Otherwise –

While he was standing in the dimness of the twilight, listening to the mutter of voices inside the tent, the girl came out again. Derry caught her wrist and stayed her.

"Look here, Molly," he said, "I want to talk to you."

"You've got a tongue, and I'm not deaf," said the girl. "Take your hands away before you break my bones."

The sunset dealt with her more gently than did candlelight. It gave to her skin a glow of delicate warmth. Her swarthiness turned to gold. In her eyes he could see the blue sheen that overlay the black.

"I'm going to see Christian," said Derry. "Shall I believe in him or not?"

"Sure you will," said the girl. "You're just that dumb."

She walked calmly away from him. Her head was high. There was a dignity about her that made it impossible for him to follow her.

11

A Talk With Christian

That next day was to see the end of Barry Christian. Therefore, the town of Blue Water was filled with people who had come scores and even hundreds of miles to attend the execution. Instead of a formal gibbet, a branch of a big spruce in the centre of the town was to serve as the lever by which Christian would be hoisted off the face of the earth and sent to his account. People loitered near the jail where the man was kept. They also lingered near the tree where he was to die. And Tom Derry rode under that tree, through the crowd, on his way to the jail.

His keen ears drank in the comments around him, as he journeyed on. He heard a man say: "Burning would be better."

He heard another man mutter: "It's a short bit of hell for Christian, but he's given some long bits to other folks."

He heard still another say: "Silver ought

to be here to see this. Silver put him in the jug, and Silver ought to see the end of him!"

So when Tom Derry reached the jail, the doubt in the back of his mind was greater than before. He wished that, the night before, he had followed Molly Cary and made her tell him exactly what she meant. But it was too late for that, now.

The jail itself was a solid fist of stone, thrust up among the frail wooden or clumsy log cabins of Blue Water. The sound of the creek hung in the air like the noise of a wind that blew all through the day and the night, in every weather.

There was a crowd in front of the jail, milling about in the street. Right at the door were four riflemen, and they were all Carys. In their patched clothes, with their unshaven faces, they looked very wild even in comparison with the people of Blue Water, who were by no means mild. Up to the door went Tom Derry and waved a hand at the guards. They brought their rifles to the ready. One of them was that fellow with the shag of black beard all over his face – Dean Cary. Another was Dean's handsome son, Will Cary. Dean pushed the muzzle of his gun right into the face of

Derry.

"Give this here jail a pile of room," said Dean Cary. "What you want?"

"The sheriff," said Derry angrily.

"Go try the side door, and maybe you'll have better luck."

So Derry went around to the side door. He found a smaller mob here, but four Carys, with rifles, were on guard. He asked his question of one of them, and the fellow turned his head and bawled:

"Hey, Sheriff!"

The door opened a bit. The sheriff's worn, hard face appeared.

"Yeah? Hello, Derry. Come on in and see the boss."

At that invitation, Derry mounted the steps and entered the jail. The sheriff said:

"He takes it pretty cool. A fellow like that Barry Christian, he ain't goin' to worry none till the breath is bein' choked out of him. And choked out it's goin' to be, this time! I got the rope, I got the tree, and I got the men that hate his heart enough to want to see him through the misery!"

How little the sheriff knew! To one who really wished to see Christian die, how much half a dozen words would mean, at this moment! That thought grew in Derry as he walked down the corridor to a corner cell, double-barred with steel. Inside those bars, like a figure in the obscurity of a blurred pencil drawing, he saw Barry Christian for the first time. He knew him perfectly, not by features, but by carriage. The dignity of a man of importance adhered to the big man. His pale, handsome face might have been that of an orator, an artist, a scientist. However big he was in body, it was plain that he was far more in mind than in muscle.

He was not chained. Instead of chains, he was secured by another quartet of the Cary clan, who sat or walked near by, their rifles in their hands, their knives and revolvers in their belts. No wiles would cut Barry Christian out of the jail unless these men were willing to have him go. It seemed madness for the sheriff to trust so blindly to the imagined hatred of the Carys for Barry Christian.

Christian lounged, reading. When the sheriff spoke, he first passed a hand through his long hair and then looked up calmly, without haste or nervousness. It was not fear that made him pale. That was plain. It was merely the natural colour of a skin that the sun could not tan.

"Is it time, Sheriff?" he asked.

"Time for you to meet a friend of mine, by name of Tom Derry," said the sheriff. He added, rather brutally: "You'll meet the other thing a little later on."

Then, turning, the sheriff drew the Cary guards along with him to a little distance, and Tom Derry stepped close to the bars.

He said loudly: "I've come here to see the size of your neck, so we can tie the hangman's knot the right size!"

Christian looked at him steadily. His voice was wonderfully soft and calm as he said: "That's not why you came, my friend. They've heard you yell at me. Now you can lower your voice and tell me the facts. Have you brought a message?"

"I've brought a message from Buck Rainey."

He saw the words take electric effect on the body, in the eyes, of Barry Christian.

"Buck Rainey?" said that magic voice of the big man. "I could have known that Buck would remember when the rest fell away."

"Have you heard anything from the guards?" asked Tom Derry.

"The guards? They've been chosen from men who hate me," said Christian.

In Derry, there was a burst of admiration for the strong discipline which had kept the Carys from letting the prisoner know that they had been bought for his cause.

"Twenty-five thousand went from Buck Rainey to the Cary tribe," he said. "I took it, and it bought the old man."

"It's a good buy at a small price," said Christian.

His perfect calmness made Derry almost smile. One thing he could tell at the beginning. No matter how many people hated Christian and loved Jim Silver, the courage of this man was perfect. And then, with the faith of Buck Rainey behind him, the passionate nature of Derry ran the entire distance and poured itself out with enthusiasm in front of Christian. Derry owed his life to Rainey. Twice he owed it, and, therefore, it was only right that he should do Rainey's bidding blindly. Moreover, there was the mission of the dead man he had left far south, behind him. He stood in the boots of that unknown now, speaking to the captive. Why doubt a man in whom Buck Rainey had belief?

He said: "The price was paid. I got the money for it from Buck Rainey. The Cary gang are your men. They would have taken

107

you out at night, but there have been other guards around at night, and the sheriff was on the job, too. It would have meant a lot of killing."

"Perfectly right," said Barry Christian. "Blood never pays, in the long run."

There was something about the small smile with which he uttered these words that froze the soul of Derry. He took in a breath and stared fixedly at the prisoner. Even now, it was not too late to change his mind, Rainey or no Rainey.

Christian said: "No matter when the Carys move for me, the cruel devils will have to be kept in hand. Who'll manage that?"

Derry sighed with relief. As for the smile that he had seen, he would find an explanation for that later on.

He said: "The old man himself is down here, and he'll keep the clan in hand."

"Good!" said Christian. "The sheriff – is he apt to be bought?"

"He can't be bought, they say. Nobody dares to try, even."

"That may save money, but it throws away chances," said Christian. "However, what's to be done?"

"They'll lead you right out to the

hanging tree," said Derry. "When you're under it, you'll be asked to speak your last words. While you're speaking, the Cary outfit will be formed around you in a circle. I'll give the word to them. By that time everyone will be waiting to see the rope tighten around your neck. You'll be on a horse, and the plan of the sheriff is to let you drop from the horse and strangle that way. Instead, that's the horse you're to ride to freedom. When I give the word, the Carys start yelling. A lot of noise helps to blind people to what's happening. They'll shoot their guns into the air. They'll make a flying wedge through the crowd, and you'll ride inside that wedge till you get a chance to bolt down the open street. I'll be riding close to you. Follow me, and I'll take you to Buck Rainey."

"Perfect!" said Barry Christian.

A terrible brightness came into his eyes as he spoke: He added: "Some of the men in Blue Water may remember today!"

"Ay," said Tom Derry. "But I hope that there'll be no killing."

Christian looked down sharply – almost as though he did not wish to have another meaning seen in his eyes.

"Of course, we hope that," he said.

"And Silver? Is Silver in town?"

"No."

"I'm thankful for that," breathed Christian. "That multiplies every chance by ten."

He feared at least one man in the world. That much was plain. The law, the crowd of enemies, meant little to him compared with the absence of Jim Silver.

"Hello!" called the sheriff, coming up. "Here's a man from New York that wants a statement out of you, Christian. Will you talk to him?"

"Why not?" answered Christian, with his usual calm. "As long as I last, I might as well be passed around from one bloodsucker to another!"

The sheriff merely laughed, and Tom Derry walked down the steel-barred aisle past a hurrying little fellow with the face of a ferret and with a pencil and paper already coming into his hand.

Outside in the open air of the morning, Derry walked into the crowd and breathed deeply of the wind. He kept telling himself that whatever Buck Rainey wanted was right. But all the while there was a bitter doubt in the back of his mind. He had tried to devote himself wholeheartedly to Barry

Christian, but something in that man's eyes filled him with doubt.

He heard someone say: "Silver oughta be here, but a man like Jim Silver does his job and never waits to be paid for it!"

Derry looked sharply at the speaker. He saw a man with a brown, open face, and fearless eyes. If ever honesty looked out of a human countenance, it looked out from that face.

And a greater doubt than ever entered Derry. He heard the heavy beat of a bell begin, and he knew it was the toll of the alarm that warned the men of Blue Water that Barry Christian was about to die.

12

The Hanging Tree

In the centre of Blue Water there was a
magnificent plaza, a space which would not
be sold to any private investor because it
was reserved for the building of the city
hall, the post office, and a few other
municipal or government buildings which
were to be an honour to the whole West!
The plans for the buildings had been
drawn. The land was bought for the
municipality. But there was not a penny on
hand to lay so much as a foundation stone.
So the big trees still grew in this open
region, and among the rest there was a
mighty silver spruce. Law had never
troubled Blue Water a great deal, but once,
in the old days, a few reputable citizens had
drawn together to form a vigilance
committee that had hanged a score or more
of rascals to that silver spruce. It was still
called the Hanging Tree, and from the
largest of its lower branches, Sheriff Walt

Milton intended to hang the great Barry Christian.

Tom Derry saw the long rope dangling, as he took his place on the fringe of the crowd which framed the Hanging Tree in a hollow square. On the outer edge of that circling group were a number of buckboards in which the occupants could stand in order to see the ceremonies better, and among the other wagons was one in which Old Man Cary sat at ease, with Maria beside him. His eyes, under their furrowed lids, were sparks of light. He smoked his pipe with slow puffs, enjoying every moment. Only the girl seemed in a cold humour, sometimes staring straight before her, sometimes looking grimly around on the faces in the crowd.

The bell was still tolling. The last arrivals were scurrying to get good places in the throng, and Derry worked his way over to the wagon of Old Man Cary. He saw that the buckboard was very light, and that the pair of mustangs which fretted between the traces looked like racers. Once a start was made, that outfit would get the old man out of harm's way about as fast as though he were a youth in the saddle. The driver would be the girl. There was plenty of strength in her, and the touch of her slender brown hands on the reins soothed the mustangs constantly. It would go hard with all that got in her way. She had the calm look of one about to do desperate things.

Derry stepped up on the hub of the wheel. The old man puffed smoke in his face and looked right through him.

"The boys are ready. I'm to give the signal," said Derry. "I yell 'Up, Cary!' and your people start to work."

"Get over into your place, then," said the old man, "and don't spoil my view."

Derry merely grinned. He said to the girl: "Still feeling as hard as a stone, Molly?"

She drew her glance gradually away from the distance and regarded him briefly.

"When you pick up a stone and throw it away, do you expect it to come back to your hand?" she asked him. "Get off that wheel before you fall off!"

He stepped down to the ground again and turned away. She seemed to hate him, just now. Perhaps she felt that he had taken her lightly. But when he came to her again, in a year or two, she would be a better age to know her own mind. And then, perhaps,

114

he could restore himself to her esteem. It was no wonder if she were inclined to sneer at him, when he reflected that with a horse or a rope or a gun she so far excelled him. As for the grimness of the old man, no doubt he was angered to think that a stranger should be in a position to give command among the Cary clan.

There was a sudden outbreak of clamour from the direction of the jail, by which he guessed that Barry Christian and his guards had come out into the open. Now he could see them slowly progressing toward the Hanging Tree. He could see a squad of four tall Carys marching first, the prisoner behind them, and more of the same clan in the rear. All about them swept a crowd of people.

Looking toward the edge of the open ground, Derry saw yet others of the clan edging forward on horseback, each of the men leading two or more horses. They were a vital part of the plan.

As the crowd now thickened, it held back, nevertheless, from the straight path which led from the jail to the Hanging Tree, and that was how Derry managed to see several things of importance, as well as to hear them.

When the prisoner was close to the Hanging Tree, an old woman squeezed through the tight wall of the spectators and tried to rush on Christian with her hands held out like claws. The guards forced her back. She yelled and screeched at them.

"Lemme at him. I'm seein' the murderer that slaughtered my two lads! Gimme a chance at him with my hands. A dog like that was never meant for hangin'. He's meant for bein' tore to pieces! Barry Christian, you murdered Ike and Lew. I seen you, and you know I seen you! You shot 'em through the back!"

She began to scream out curses till her voice cracked and went out. She fell back into arms that carried her away to the open air.

As Barry Christian moved on, a tall old man said loudly, calmly:

"It's a day I've been watchin' and prayin' for for ten years, Barry Christian. I'm Hank Mason, from Texas. You recollect me, you blood-suckin' rat? It ain't money you've lived on. It's blood and humans!"

There were other voices raised, here and there, but they were lost in one great, general cry of execration that swelled every throat in the mob, it seemed. And poor

116

Tom Derry was stunned. Had he undertaken labour, faced danger, and was he now about to make his own head wanted by the law all for the sake of a man who richly deserved hanging?

He had to harken back to the voice of Buck Rainey, and to tell himself that Rainey must be right and all the rest wrong.

Now the procession arrived at the proper spot under the tree when a slender man of middle height or less pushed through the crowd. He said to a bulky fellow:

"Give me a hand up so that the people can see me, will you?"

"Sure, Taxi," said the cowpuncher. "You can stand on my neck any time you want to."

The name had riveted the attention of Derry on the stranger. He had heard, from Rainey, of Silver's closest adherent and most faithful friend. He looked with amazement on this slender youth with a handsome face.

When "Taxi" looked down, he might have passed for the most innocuous man in the world. It was only when he looked up that men could see the pale, bright danger in his eyes, that old battle light which is recognized by instinct and fear, if not by experience. This was the man, it was said, who had walked through the heaviest and most complicated locks as though he carried a key in his hand; this was the man who would give his life as freely as a gesture for the sake of Jim Silver.

Well, Silver might command the devotion of a few friends, thought Tom Derry, but that did not prove that he was a good man.

"Hey, folks!" yelled the big cattleman who was holding up Taxi. "Hey, here's Taxi that wants to say a word to you!"

"Taxi!" shouted the crowd instantly. "Hi, Taxi, boy! Where's Jim Silver? Where's Silver? Why ain't he here? Silver! Silver!"

The uproar fell like thunder on the ears of Tom Derry. He could not and he would not believe what he heard. The applause of a few people was not apt to mean a great deal, but when an entire crowd cheers, it is a different matter. And wherever he looked, he could see men waving their hats, actually jumping up and down as they yelled in honour of Jim Silver.

Taxi, looking over this demonstration without a smile, lifted a hand that instantly

118

cut the roaring in two and brought a silence.

Then he said in a quiet but incisive voice: "I've had word that a rescue is going to be attempted here today. I'm here to tell the men who may have the rescue idea in mind that I and three others are going to be standing with drawn guns. The instant that there's a move to free Barry Christian, we've sworn to shoot Christian first; afterwards we'll try to handle the rescuers in the same way."

He was lowered to the ground, while a single deep shout of rage and apprehension went up from the bystanders.

But Tom Derry was stunned again. It seemed to him that everything that had been accomplished was at this moment reduced to nothingness. Staring blankly around him, he could pick out the men who would send their bullets into Christian the instant that a disturbance commenced. He could pick them out by their drawn guns – one with a rifle, and the other three, including Taxi, with revolvers or automatics. And the crowd fell back from these men a trifle, so as to give them room.

Last of all, Tom Derry stared at Christian, wondering whether this could be, after all, a man worth the risk of life and soul. He saw Christian standing under the Hanging Tree with the noose end of the long rope dangling near his head. That head was carried high. The pale face of the prisoner seemed about to smile. He had the look of one about to speak to an assemblage of dear friends who would burst into applause at his first words. But his hands were tied behind his back, and his shirt collar was unbuttoned, exposing the soft of his throat about which the strangling rope was intended to close.

Another picture of a man equally calm in the face of danger – burned clearly into the inward vision of Derry. And again he was sure. Whatever the crowd felt, Barry Christian must be right, and all the others were wrong. All the others – and Silver – and Taxi – they were wrong, and Barry Christian was worth the risk of a life.

Big Dean Cary was standing not far away, and now he stepped close to Derry, muttering:

"The goose is cooked, and the game's finished. We can't do a thing."

Derry answered softly: "We can still make a try – and win!" He added: "There aren't many guns in this outfit. The men

120

have turned out to see an execution, not to take part in a fight. That's where we have the edge. Taxi and the other three – we have them spotted. One of us has to take a stand on each side of the four. There are plenty of us for the job. When I yell: 'Up, Cary!' we grab our men. I'll catch at Taxi's gun hand. You crack him behind the ear. Not to kill, mind you. Don't use the butt, but the barrel of your gun. Lay him out. Pass on the word to the rest of the boys. Get 'em in their posts. I'll pass the same word along. Dean, we've got to win out on this job."

He heard a long breath exhaled from the lips of Dean Cary.

"You've got the nerve of a devil, kid!" said the big man, and he glided off to the side.

A big black horse was brought – the same one which had been ridden by Derry in Cary Valley. Barry Christian was forced to mount it.

Sheriff Walt Milton stood by with the noose of the hangman's rope in his hand. He said: "Speak your piece, Barry. We ain't got much time now!"

Christian looked over the crowd. Last of all, his glance found the tense face of Tom

Derry and dwelt there for an instant. It seemed to Derry that whatever Christian said would be spoken primarily for his ears, and he was eager to know what the words would be.

The speech was not long. Barry Christian simply said: "My friends, I – "

He got that far when a voice yelled: "Not friends, blast you!"

Sheriff Walt Milton called out: "Quiet, boys, and let him talk. He ain't got much time for many words."

"My friends," said Barry Christian, "I have done some bad things in my life, and it seems that most of you know about them. But I suppose that most people have done bad things, now and then. If you say that I ought to die, I won't deny it. I'll say this to excuse myself – that I've been straight with my friends and hard on my enemies."

A deep rumbling of rage came out of the throats of the crowd.

"And when I wait here for death," went on Christian, "I have the feeling that no matter what my enemies may be, my friends are worth more. I'm not sending any messages out. The people that hate me have enough when they've throttled me with a rope. The people who love me don't need a last message. Sheriff, go ahead with your work!"

And he turned and looked down at Walt Milton.

It was enough for Tom Derry. Every fibre of his honest nature was burning with belief in the prisoner by this time. His lips parted over the cry: "Up, Cary!" and at the same instant he grasped the gun hand of Taxi and bore the gun down out of the line that pointed towards Christian.

A stream of lead spattered out of the automatic into the ground. Taxi whirled on Derry. A big man and a powerful man was Derry, but he felt that he had laid hands on a wildcat that would rip him to pieces. Then he saw the flash of Dean Cary's gun. The barrel of it clanged with a dull sound against the base of Taxi's skull, and he slithered down into the dust, lying in a heap.

Other hands fell on Derry then, as the enraged townsmen reached for him. He tore himself free, fighting. His fists won a little opening for him, and into that opening the rescue charged.

It was all very neat, the plan he had built up. Taxi and his three friends of the guns had gone down at the first yell of "Up,

Cary!" The rest of the Cary clan inside the circle had made Barry Christian a free man and a fighting unit by slashing the ropes that held his arms behind his back and by putting revolvers into his hands. And the horse from which he was to have been hanged was now the power that might carry him away to freedom.

At the same time, while the crowd began to show guns, here and there, the men of Blue Water heard the familiar yell ringing from the rear all around the outskirts, where man after man of the clan was bringing in the horses. "Up, Cary!" they shouted at the full of their power, and the townsmen could see the heads of the plunging mustangs and hear the squealing of the broncos as they were spurred and flogged forward. At the same time, from around the freed prisoner, from the very point where law seemed most secure, from the very clansmen who had been trusted to guard Christian, they heard the same wild yelling.

"Up, Cary!" And guns were firing rapidly from all directions.

It hardly mattered that those bullets flew high in the air. The important thing was that they made a noise. The crowd began to shudder and then to melt. Sheriff Walt Milton was tapped over the head, and his hands were tied behind his back, and then the horses came pouring into the open space beneath the Hanging Tree. In a moment the Carys were mounted. They formed into a flying wedge with Tom Derry at the point of it, and Barry Christian in the centre. That was the way they hit the men of Blue Water and ploughed a way out to freedom. And as they got into the street, when a rousing gallop was possible, Tom Derry saw the buckboard of the old man sweeping away in a cloud of its own dust. He knew it was the old man's outfit, for he could see Maria Cary standing erect on the driver's footboard and throwing the whip into the horses as they sprinted. And the buckboard leaped and flung like a fish on a hook, behind the rapid heels of the mustangs.

13

Outlawed

Outside of the town, the Carys melted to this side and that, and waved and shouted farewells as they disappeared in groups among the rocks and the trees. What would happen to them in their valley, now? Would Walt Milton gather the force of the law behind himself and enter the valley and send the whole wild crew to prison?

It could be done, undoubtedly. It seemed far more possible now that Tom Derry had in mind and memory the deep hate of the crowd in Blue Water for Barry Christian. They would want to leave no stone unturned to get at the rascals who had double-crossed the sheriff and set the prisoner free.

But the valley was, after all, far away, and hard to win. It would cost a great deal of blood. There was still a chance that the Carys might continue their pastoral life until the last of their mob crimes had been

126

forgotten if not forgiven.

So the flying rout dwindled, rather suddenly, to no more than Tom Derry and his famous companion.

Barry Christian said: "It took brains and it took nerve and a pair of hands. Nobody but you could have done that job, Tom Derry."

His voice was grave, and his eyes were deeply considerate. Tom felt that he had been praised by a king of men.

"When I saw that venomous devil of a Taxi," said Christian, "I was sure that it was the end. He almost never fails. He carries within an ounce as much poison as Silver has."

"Who is Taxi?" said Derry. "I've heard a little about him but not much. I'm new to this part of the country."

"Not very new, if you know Rainey," said Christian, smiling, his eyes very keen above the smile.

"Rainey is all I *do* know," said Derry. "I don't even know why the Blue Water men wanted to hang you – except that Jim Silver had railroaded you into some trouble."

Christian cleared his throat. "Is that all Rainey told you?" he asked, in a somewhat constrained voice.

"That's all, and I've had no time to ask questions. But what is Taxi?"

"Taxi," said Christian, "is a gutter rat. He came out of New York because even that big town got too hot to hold him. Since then he's been floating about, here and there, mostly here, with Silver. Taxi knows what any first class yegg is always glad to know – how to pick a lock and how to blow a safe. He carries a set of picklocks around with him all the time."

"Why did the people cheer for him then?" asked Derry, somewhat bewildered.

"Ah, that's because he belongs to Silver."

"And how does Silver hypnotize people, if he's such a crook?"

Christian laughed, but his eyes wandered a trifle.

"If Silver would tell his secret," said Christian, "we'd all be a lot wiser. But he's simply the world's greatest hypocrite!"

"Ay, and that's what Rainey told me," agreed Tom Derry, more and more convinced. "Besides," he added, "I don't need any convincing. Only, when I heard the mob yell against you – you know how it is – it shook me up a little."

"I saw that it did," said Christian.

"When I saw your face change, I could almost feel the rough of the rope around my neck."

He laughed again, but added soberly: "The best of it all is that Taxi's dead and done for! Without him, Silver is only a one-handed man, so to speak."

"Taxi is not dead," said Derry. "I only let Dean Cary give him the barrel of a revolver along the head. He'll sleep five minutes and wake up with a goose egg on the back of his skull. That's all."

"Not dead?" cried Christian. "You mean to say that when you had a chance – you mean to say that you didn't kill Taxi?"

"Why, man, it would have been murder!" said Derry, opening his eyes.

Christian said savagely: "It will be another kind of murder when Taxi runs you down on your trail. And that's a trail that he'll never leave unless Silver calls him off it. He'll have you, one of these days, and he'll have you hard! When he slides his knife into your throat – you'll have time to think one thought, maybe, before you choke and die! Murder? What will you call it when you hear your door opening in the dark of your room and know that something had crawled in over the

129

threshold? That'll be Taxi – and that'll be the way you die, my friend! Murder? You'll know more about murder before that gutter rat is through with you!"

The words came out of Christian in such a bitter storm that Derry was half overwhelmed.

He could only mutter: "Well, it would have meant taking him by surprise – with his head turned. I – I couldn't kill a man like that."

"You couldn't?" asked Christian.

"No, and I don't suppose that you could either," answered Tom Derry.

Christian smiled, and the smile was almost a sneer.

"You may learn some new things before you're much older, Tom," he said. "You may learn that when it comes to hunting certain kinds of birds, the only safe way is to be a cat." He went on sombrely: "Not that I like it. I loathe it. But I have to play the game the way Silver lays down the rules!"

Tom Derry said nothing. He merely shook his head.

For his part, he was beginning to be sorry that he had taken upon himself the duty of keeping another man's rendezvous.

He had met Buck Rainey and owed his life to that man. He had met this strange and powerful nature, Barry Christian. But for all that, he began to wish that he had remained in more obscure paths of life, no matter how often he stumbled upon danger.

He was outlawed, by this time. His description was being passed across the range by word of mouth. In every little post office, there would soon appear a placard offering some sort of a reward for "information leading to the apprehension of Thomas Derry." Perhaps there would remain for him no refuge except the wilds of Cary Valley, where he would have to live among those savages, in rags and tatters.

Or, perhaps, the end would be what Christian had prophesied – a knife in the slender, swift hand of Taxi, and the point of it driven into Tom Derry's throat.

He fell into a long silence, automatically leading the way across hills and through the ravines toward the place where they must find Buck Rainey – now doubtless well able to sit the saddle.

But as Derry rode, a new and darker trouble came over his mind. For it seemed to him that he could feel the glance of Barry

131

Christian repeatedly upon him, with a covert sneer lingering in the look of the big man. And the great doubt returned.

14

The Parting

Outside the grove where Rainey had last been seen, Derry shouted. Almost instantly Rainey's whistle answered him, and Derry rode with Christian in among the trees. They found Rainey brushing down the velvet black hide of his mare, Nell. He did not come to greet them. He merely seemed to pause in his work, as he turned and waved.

"Good to see you, Barry," he called, as he waved his hand.

Christian dismounted. To be sure, he shook the hand of Rainey, but it seemed no more than a casual gesture. It was such a greeting as two men might have given each other after parting the night before.

"How does the leg go?" asked Christian.

"Pretty well," said Rainey. "Hungry, Barry?"

"Hungry enough to eat. Got anything?"

"Venison," said Rainey exultantly.

"That fawn sneaked in here among the trees, this morning, and I just had time to put a slug through it."

He pointed to a dappled skin which hung at a corner of the clearing, hauled up to a branch of a tree.

"If you can do that," said Christian, "you can ride."

"I can ride better than I can walk," said Rainey.

"Then ride now," said Christian. "We'll cut up some of that meat and take it along with us."

"What's the rush? asked Rainey.

"Silver always makes a rush," said Christian.

"Silver?" exclaimed Buck Rainey. "What brought that devil into the talk?"

"The whole of Blue Water is out on our trail," said Christian.

"Why, that's nothing," answered Rainey.

"No, but Taxi's with the rest of 'em."

"Taxi?" shouted Rainey, and his hand went instinctively to a gun.

"He was there to see my neck properly stretched," answered Christian, "and now he's on the trail. And wherever Taxi, is, he knows how to raise the ghost of Silver out

134

of the ground. You know that!"

"Know it? Of course, I know it!" exclaimed Rainey. "Let's get moving!"

He had a saddle on Nell in no time, and away the three of them went across the country, leaving the venison hanging behind them.

They travelled hard all that afternoon. Once or twice the face of Rainey seemed pinched with pain from his wound, but this passed quickly, and he was as cheerful as the other two at the end of the afternoon. They halted late in the evening, in woods close to water. The first thing was the dressing of Rainey's wound. It was only a trifle inflamed, and had endured the travel very well indeed. Christian attended to the fresh dressing, and Derry started the cookery.

Afterward, they sat around the coals of the fire, almost always silent. The whole afternoon of riding had been nearly wordless, also. But that was not strange. It is the habit of men on the trail in the West to speak very little. The dust and the labour are enough to keep tongues quiet. But it was odd that the two old friends did not commune more freely when they sat by the campfire. There was only one moment of much conversation, and that was entirely on the part of Christian, who described in much detail, to Rainey, how Derry had talked to him in the jail, and how perfectly the plan had gone through, in spite of the presence of Taxi.

When the narrative ended, Rainey smiled, and looked at Christian.

"I wasn't sending you a fool or a blind man, Barry," he said. "The luck was that Silver didn't show up at Blue Water to see the hanging."

"He wouldn't do it," Christian sneered, his pale face twisting a little with the intensity of his hatred. "He wouldn't descend that far. The perfect man, Buck, is never seen gloating over a fallen enemy. Besides, Silver is too busy to come to a hanging."

"Busy catching rabbits, maybe?" Rainey chuckled.

That bit of talk did not please Derry much. From ordinary men he would have received it with a great deal of suspicion, but from these two, both of whom he felt were much his superiors in mind, he felt that he could take much and reserve his opinion. So he endured the talk, only frowning down at the dying fire until the words ceased. Suddenly, and when he looked up, he had a feeling that a glance had passed between his two companions.

He was very tired, so he went to sleep almost immediately, giving one twist of a blanket about him as he lay down. His eyes closed, and he was gone.

It was hours later when he wakened suddenly. There had been no sound. The moonlight lay white on the grass of the clearing, and one thin twist of smoke was rising from the ashes of the fire into the moonshine, but off to the side he saw Christian and Rainey talking together, seated side by side.

They were sufficiently far away so that by guarding their voices not even a murmur reached the ears of Derry. The only significance to him was in the gestures, and the way the heads of the men were put close together. Whatever they were talking over, it was of a great deal of importance to them. Rainey carried the lead, and now and again he drew on the moonlit ground little plans, which he afterward carefully erased. These plans Christian always stooped over and scrutinized with the utmost care. And finally, he made a swift gesture, high over his head, an unmistakable sign of triumph.

Derry turned his head and closed his eyes. He had a feeling that he had eavesdropped, and he could not help the sense that he had overlooked a guilty moment.

What could the guilt be? One thing was almost sure to him – if there were one vital thing wrong with these two men, then everything about them was wrong, and the crowd in Blue Water had been right when it cheered Taxi and Jim Silver and snarled like a great thousand-throated beast at Barry Christian.

But the two men could not be wrong, he told himself; Buck Rainey, at least, had proved himself capable of risking his life for a friend, even for a new friend.

The problem made a sad confusion in the mind of Derry. He was not a splitter of hairs or a great thinker. He decided, on this occasion, that all his manhood demanded that he should follow Rainey blindly, no matter where the trail took him.

On that decision he fell asleep again.

In the morning there was a quick breakfast of coffee and hardtack. Then they saddled. Christian said:

"Derry, will you ride over to Little Rock for me?"

"I'll ride to Little Rock," answered Derry, "even if you mean Arkansas."

"Not that far. North-east, through the hills. I'll draw the trail for you. Go to Little Rock, or in sight of it. Just over the town you'll find a bald-headed hill with just one tuft of forest in the centre of it. Go up on that hill and wait in those woods till you get word. You'll reach Little Rock inside of two days, I suppose."

"What's the main idea?" asked Derry.

"The main idea," said Rainey, "is to have a man on the spot to get a message from us. If you see a man with a rag of white tied on his left bridle rein, you'll know that he's our messenger. Is that clear?"

"Clear as day," said Derry.

"If you need money," said Rainey, "here's a few hundred."

He took out his wallet and picked from it a few greenbacks. The size of the denominations made the eyes of Derry enlarge. He stared at the money without moving a hand.

"It's yours," said Rainey, smiling.

Derry took in a quick, gulping breath. Then he smiled in turn and shook his head. His breath exploded with the words:

"Can't take it, Buck. Thanks, but I can't take it. I've been on the bum, I know, but I never took a hand-out that I didn't work for. I've never taken a penny in my life that I didn't earn."

"Why, man," exclaimed Buck Rainey, "haven't you been working for Barry Christian – and me?"

"Working?" said Derry, opening his honest eyes wide. "I thought I was just helping out a friend – I thought I was doing something to help you, Buck. I wasn't doing it for pay."

As he stared, the glance of Rainey flickered away to the side. Apparently it crossed that of Barry Christian before it returned to Derry, and this angered Derry, he could hardly have said why.

"Have you any money at all?" asked Rainey.

"I have enough," answered Derry, frowning.

"All right, then," said Rainey. "Let it go that way." He added, with a sudden increase of heartiness: "I understand your feeling. But it's not often that we run across your sort of man, Tom. So long. See you before long."

Christian and Rainey both shook hands

in parting. Then Christian said:

"Here, Tom. Take that black I've been riding. He's worth ten of your mustang."

It touched Derry, both the offer and the hearty, casual way in which it was made.

"And what about you?" he asked with concern.

"About me? Oh, I'll pick up another horse that's as good or better before the day's out. While the law hounds are after me, I'll have to have good horseflesh between my knees. But I'll find another mount in three hours."

That was how Tom Derry happened to find himself possessed of the black horse on which Barry Christian had fled from Blue Water, and such was the unsuspicious nature of his mind that he mounted it without a single misgiving, and while he waved to his two departing acquaintances, he gloried in the long, free stride of the fine horse that was to bring such danger to his trail.

15

A Grey Wolf

All through that day he saw no human being. He travelled through huge, broken country. Sometimes in one valley the north slope was soft and green and the south slope was covered with dry grass on which the sun flashed and the wind rustled. There were grass regions and forested places. He climbed above timber line and drifted among the bee pastures. He had a view from the highlands of lakes sunk in deep gorges, like great blue eyes.

By one of those lakes he camped. The yellow of his firelight turned the little waves of the lake to ripples of gold over the black. He could not see the tops of the images of the trees. And as the wind came and went busily through the woods, he asked himself what a man wanted more in the world than a chance to let his eye grasp, every day, all that was held within the round of such a Western horizon.

He suddenly felt calmer and steadier, and wondered why the wanderlust had left his blood within so few days! When he reached back into his mind to find the reason, his thought struck on the image of "Molly Cary." There it lodged. He had found his mate, and one day he would go for her. He would find a way to make her come happily with him. He would take up a land claim, somewhere in this region, this same district of the Blue Waters. He would fell logs, and they would build a cabin. The earth and their labours would support them.

He was full of that thought when he lay wrapped in his blanket. The last thing he knew was the leap of a fish, breaking water in the lake.

When he wakened, the morning was commencing about him, and he let his eye run up the tall shafts of the trees into the thin, bright blue of the sky.

Where the lake broke into ripples, running out down a little creek, he caught trout and breakfasted on them when they were broiled brown. Then he mounted the black horse and went on his way according to the map that was planned and drawn in his mind. The day was still and bright and

143

hot in the hollows, clear and delightful on the uplands. It was on the uplands, somewhere, that he would build his cabin. If there were wind, he would not mind. It is best to have movement, even in the sky.

Late in the afternoon, from a great height, from the verge of a tall-shouldered bulwark of mountains, he looked down on Little Rock and saw the circle of hills, and particularly that one which was crowned with what seemed a mere scalp-lock of woods. That was his destination.

He was about to go on, across the big valley that lay between him and his goal, when he felt eyes behind him, and looked quickly around in time to see a great grey timber wolf disappearing into a clump of brush.

He pulled his revolver and waited for a second glimpse, but the animal was gone. And he chuckled. How could men live in cities when there was real life to be found out here in the wilderness, where the watcher is watched?

He rode on down the valley, sent the tired black gelding up the slope of his promised hill, and came to the circling woods that crowned it. It was a perfect camping place, with a clearing inside the hollow circle of the trees, and a small spring breaking out in the midst of the open place. There was plenty of tall grass for the black to graze, and when he had picketed the horse, he found enough daylight remaining to survey his surroundings carefully before he had supper of hardtack and coffee.

From the one side, he looked down into the town of Little Rock. It got its name from a great boulder that rose in the centre of the little frame buildings, all flashing with the western light that struck the windows. A huge rock loomed up the valley at a small distance. When he had considered the town for a moment, through the thin smoke haze that drifted over it, he rounded the hill slowly, keeping to the edge of the woods, and from the opposite side looked down the slope he had mounted. There, gliding from one patch of brush to another, he had a longer look at the same grey wolf that he had seen earlier in the afternoon.

He knew it was the same one, because a man would not see two of that size in an entire lifetime. Besides, the beast was distinguished by the light dusty grey of its colour, perfectly fitted to melt into a background of sand or of rocks or of

145

sunburned foliage. The timber wolf felt the glance of the human eye. Instead of slinking off, it sat down and opened its mouth and favoured him with a bit of blood-red laughter.

He felt a chill up his spine. Also, he had a desire to laugh. So he compromised between the two emotions by snatching out a revolver. The lobo waited not an instant, but sprang into the brush and was gone. It would not come out again; he knew the uncanny wisdom of the race.

So he went back and had his supper in the darkening of the day. He was on his second cup of night-black coffee when something stirred soundlessly. In the tail of his eye he saw the dim silhouette of his friend the grey wolf!

The fear that had come faintly upon him at his second meeting with the brute was an electric shock at this third encounter. He could not move a hand for a moment, then he rose slowly to his feet. But to his bewilderment, the wolf did not budge! Instead, it crouched as though ready to hurl itself at him!

He had heard of wolves attacking humans, though he had never actually known an eye-witness of such an occurrence. But in every case, the wolf was supposed to be driven half mad by the pangs of the winter famine, whereas this big fellow seemed in the perfect pink of condition. And there was the lobo in leaping distance, while he, Tom Derry, was three steps from the spot where he had foolishly left his revolver!

There was the light hand axe near him, but he wondered if it would be safe to lean for it.

Then, behind him, the deep voice of a man said: "You can hoist your hands. Put them up, mind you!"

He felt that voice through him. There was such authority that though he was a fighting man by pride and by instinct, he found his hands obeying the command.

They went up as high as his shoulders, as high as his ears.

"Turn this way," said the commanding voice. It added: "It's not Christian, Taxi. Come on in. We wouldn't have such luck."

From the other side of the clearing came the voice of Taxi: "What good if it were Christian, anyway? You wouldn't do anything about him. You'd simply turn him back to the law again, Jim."

"Turn around!" commanded the first

speaker.

Derry turned gradually. He hated to give his back to that crouched devil of a wolf. It seemed as if the man with the deep voice read his thoughts perfectly, because he said:

"The wolf won't hurt you. Not if you move slowly. Frosty – steady, boy!"

Then, as Derry faced about, he saw a big man step from behind a tree into the thin red of the firelight. One did not need full day to see his formidable size, the weight of his shoulders, and the look of speed and lightness about the rest of him. It was Jim Silver, of course. He, and Taxi – and the wolf, Frosty, of which people had spoken more than once. There was only Parade lacking, the golden chestnut of which people talked still more. Then the trio would be complete.

There was a gun in the hand of Silver, held negligently at his side.

"Tie his hands," commanded Silver.

The hands of Derry were suddenly pulled down behind his back by one who had approached with a soundless step. A hard twist of cord fastened his wrists together.

"Take a look at him," said Silver. "You

148

remember faces, Taxi. I don't think I've seen this fellow before."

"He's the one who gave the signal the other day at Blue Water. He must be one of Christian's inside men. He has to be, or he wouldn't be on Christian's horse, pulling the scent away from the chief thug of them all!"

Derry could see the truth of that, and it stunned him. Christian had confessed that he expected Silver on the trail before long. What better way, then, of throwing the hunt of Silver astray than by giving his horse with its known tracks to another man? It might be that that had not been in the mind of Christian, but the thing seemed strangely close to the probability. It could not be the truth, however, because Buck Rainey would not let a friend be imposed upon even by a greater friend. He had to pin his faith to Rainey.

"You belong to Christian, do you?" said Silver.

"I don't belong to him," answered Derry. "I never saw him before Blue Water."

"You lie," said Taxi.

"Don't do that, Taxi," cautioned Silver.

"Bah," said Taxi, "when I see the

snakes, I want to cut their throats. Look at him! He's willing to ride Christian's horse and lead the hunt crooked, and he's fool enough to think that the money he gets can be worth the risk. Nobody knows what he was paid for the job in Blue Water."

"What were you paid?" asked Silver.

"Nothing," said Derry.

"Search him," said Silver.

Taxi's lightning fingers went rapidly through the clothes of Derry and brought out the thin wallet.

"Eighteen dollars and some chicken feed," said Taxi.

"That's strange," remarked Silver. "What's your name?"

"Tom Derry."

"Sit down here by the fire, please."

"Jim," said Taxi savagely, "are you going to waste time on him? We've got to make him tell us where Christian can be found."

"All right," answered Silver. "Will you tell us where we can find Christian, Derry?"

"I don't know where he is," said Derry.

"Ah, you don't know?"

"He lies, of course," said Taxi. "I'm going to put pressure on the big rat!"

"No, not that," said Silver. "I don't want any of that."

"You don't want that? No, you want to fight fair – with snakes!" cried Taxi. "I'm going to ask for my own chance, though. It is fair to *me* if you let these hounds that Christian hires get through your hands time after time? They're after you. They're always after you. They'd knife you or bomb you in the dark. They'd poison a whole river if they thought you'd be one of the dead. But you still treat them like human beings. Jim, they'll get you, and they'll get me, unless you change your tactics."

Silver turned his back.

"Do what you please, then," he consented, and stepped over by the fire.

"Now," said Taxi to Derry, "are you talking?"

"I've nothing to say," answered Derry.

Even by the dim light, he could see the devil flare in the eyes and twist at the face of Taxi.

"You crooked me the other day in Blue Water," he said. "Now I'll see how I can loosen your tongue for you."

He took another length of cord out of his pocket and twisted it around the head of Derry. Into the loop of the cord above one

151

ear he thrust the barrel of his automatic. Derry knew what that meant. A twisting, tightening cord like that would cut through the flesh to the bone, in time. Before that, it crushed the eyes out. He drew in a slow breath and prepared to endure.

"I'm giving you your last chance," said Taxi. "If you won't talk—— "

"I won't talk," said Derry.

"Then take it!" said Taxi, and gave the automatic the first turn, taking up the slack.

"Wait a minute," said the voice of Silver, who had not turned from the dying fire.

"Walk away. Keep away out of hearing," urged Taxi. "Let me have five minutes with him, and I'll make him talk or know the reason why!"

"Sorry, partner," said Silver. "I can't walk away. I can't stand it."

The words sounded very strange in the ears of Derry. It was not the sort of thing he expected to hear from the fiend who had pursued Christian with such malice and hate.

"Once more!" groaned Taxi. "Are you going to lie down and let them walk over you?"

"I'm sorry," said Silver. "You may be

152

right – but I can't stand it!"

Taxi snatched the cord from the head of Derry and flung it on the ground.

"We're beaten before we start!" he said. "Your squeamishness will always beat us. We've cornered him more than once. He ought to be dead long ago. But he's still alive because you won't treat him for what he is – a dog!"

Silver said nothing, but the long silence began to send a chill and a thrill through the soul of Tom Derry. For the first time he confronted firmly the possibility that Buck Rainey might be wrong about this man.

16

Silver's Decision

Silver whistled. At once there was a light trampling beyond the trees. It came closer. Out of the brush stepped a horse that gleamed like copper wherever the firelight touched its body. Only a stallion could have such a head and neck, and a stallion is about as tractable as a panther. But this monster went straight up to Silver and stood obviously at attention. Yet Tom Derry could see clearly that the big horse wore not a bridle and bit, but simply a light halter with a pair of reins attached to it!

Then he realized that that must be the Parade of whom he had heard men speak. The grey wolf, at the appearance of the horse, showed every sign of hate and rage. It crouched in front of its master and bared its teeth and snarled in a consummate fury. But Parade lowered his head and sniffed at Frosty with prickling ears and a fearless curiosity.

"Frosty is going to tear his throat wide open for him, one of these days," declared that gloomy prophet, Taxi. "He hates Parade. You ought to see that, Jim."

"Frosty won't touch him. Not as long as I'm alive," said Silver.

He sat down on a rock by the fire and took off his sombrero. The reddish light showed to Derry a brown, handsome, rather weary face. He could not guess at the exact age, for as Silver turned, his expression altered. Sometimes he seemed not more than twenty-five. Again, he looked ten years older.

Above his temples, Derry could see the two tufts of grey hair, like incipient horns. They gave a hint of something devilish, like an uncanny image out of a fable.

"You think," went on Taxi, who was plainly in a state of high irritation, "that there's nothing in the way of danger for Parade from Frosty – while you live? You think you can control the teeth of Frosty even when your back is turned?"

"I think that what I've handled has scent on it. He won't touch that scent with his teeth. Is that so strange?"

"Have it your way, then," muttered Taxi. "You always do! But now tell me what we're to do about this Christian. He's back there, by this time – back there with his Duff Gregor and his Buck Rainey and the rest of his cut-throats and sneaks and blood-suckers."

It was too much for Tom Derry. He exclaimed:

"That's a lie, Taxi, and you know it. Buck Rainey is the straightest man in the world."

"Lie?" snapped Taxi, spinning around.

Then he seemed to realize that the hands of the prisoner were tied.

"You mean that Buck Rainey's not a yegg and a thief and a confidence man?" asked Taxi calmly.

"He's not!" said Derry, "and the man who says he is, is a hound!"

"Jim," murmured Taxi, "I'm going to turn this fellow loose, and we'll have it out together.

"Just a moment," interrupted Silver. "What makes you so sure that Rainey's an honest man, Derry?"

"I owe my life to him, twice over," answered Derry. "Besides, I'd swear by him and die for him. A whiter man was never born!"

"Are you swallowing that, Jim?" asked

Taxi, aside.

"I'm thinking it over," replied Silver. "How long have you know Rainey?"

"Only a few days, but every day has had years packed into it."

"He talks like a fool as well as a crook," said Taxi, and Derry could see the pale brightness of the eyes with which Taxi regarded him.

"Will you tell me how Buck Rainey saved your life?" asked Silver. Again Tom Derry marvelled, not at the words, but at the gentleness and the courtesy of the voice.

"I'll tell you," said Derry. "Once, when I was hanging head down on a barbed-wire fence and a bull was coming at me as fast as he could spread himself. And another time a gang was after me, and Rainey, instead of riding away – he was on a fast horse – turned back and opened up on that crew with his gun, and gave me my chance to get clear away. They put some lead in him to pay for it. And now you want me to stand here and let you call him a crook?"

Indignation made his voice ring.

"Taxi," said Silver, "turn him loose."

"Turn him – you mean, to set him free?" cried Taxi.

"Yes," said Silver.

"Set him free so that I can have it out with him?" pleaded Taxi.

"What chance would he have against you?" asked Silver, rather sternly. "No, but give him his horse and let him go."

"Are you out of your head?" demanded Taxi. "He's a fighting man, I tell you. It's he that set Christian free. He's the one who gave——"

"Never mind," said Silver. "I'm working a little in the dark, I admit, but I know that in the long run no honest man can be of any use to Christian."

"You call this one honest?" demanded Taxi.

Silver nodded as he answered: "He's honest. He's honest enough to do a lot of harm to Christian before the game is ended. So turn him loose."

Taxi, cursing under his breath, obeyed. Tom Derry swung his free hands forward and looked down at them in amazement.

"There's your horse," remarked Silver. "Take him and go where you please."

Tom Derry saddled the black horse of Barry Christian, and his hands moved as in a trance, without wit or sense in them. His brain was a blank. At last, standing at the

158

head of his horse, he looked across at Silver and saw the big man stripping away the saddle from Parade, taking even the halter off, to let the monster run free. It seemed to Derry that a man who could trust a dumb beast to this extent could be trusted by other men. And he could not help breaking out:

"Silver, I know from Buck Rainey what you are. But no matter what comes of it, I want you to try to count on me after this!"

"Ay," said Taxi bitterly, "count you among Christian's guns!"

But Silver called cheerfully: "Thanks, Derry. Good luck."

That was all. And then Derry rode from the trees, and was surprised to find the white of moonlight silvering the ground of the hillside. His brain had been too filled, during the last moments, to permit him to look far above the ground.

As he rode down toward the town of Little Rock, he saw another horseman coming up toward him. He came closer, and Derry saw that it was a very big fellow with a hump of strength across his shoulders. He had a surprisingly small mustang under him. Next of all, Derry marked a white rag that fluttered on the bridle rein of the stranger.

He rode straight to the big fellow, and when he came close, he exclaimed with a shock of terror and a wild relief:

"Stan Parker!"

"Sure," said the rider. "Sure, sure! Did I throw a shock into you, kid? You thought you'd done me in, down there in Cleve's saloon, didn't you? Well, you knocked the wind right out of me, and I still got a plaster across my ribs. But that ain't nothin'. I come along here to fetch you. Buck Rainey sent me. How's things?"

"Turn your horse around and tin-can out of here as fast as you can," urged Tom Derry, "because there's worse trouble up there in the trees than you think about."

"What kind of trouble?" asked Stan Parker.

"Jim Silver and Taxi," said Derry.

He expected to make an effect, but he did not expect to see Stan Parker doubled up by the news, then spread out along the back of the mustang, which he was spurring with might and main, looking back as though the air were already full of bullets. Derry shook his head, and followed him at a rapid gallop.

17

The Cary Outfit

Stan Parker kept up his speed until he was far on the other side of Little Rock. Then he pulled up on a highland that permitted him to look far behind them toward possible danger of pursuit. Here Derry overtook him.

"Not that there's much use," panted Parker, pulling off his hat and mopping his face with his sleeve, "If Silver wants to get you, he gets you. It ain't much use runnin' like that."

"Well, he's only a man," said Tom Derry. "One slug of lead would stop him, wouldn't it?"

You try it," urged Parker. "I don't want none of it. I've known gents that had the same idea about Silver. I've known fellows that went out and tried to slam him and get famous, that way. But they never come to no good. *You* try it, Tom. I don't want no part of Jim Silver."

161

He mopped his face again, pulled out a flask, took a long swig at it, and proffered a drink to his companion.

"No," said Derry. "Not until I'm out of these woods. No whisky. It snarls up a man's eye too much. About Silver, I'm not saying that I want trouble with him. I'm tired of trouble. But – where are we heading now?"

Parker took another swig from the flask. Then he said:

"I still got a shudder in the back of my brain. Silver and Taxi together, eh? That's bad enough to give any man the willies. Where are we heading? For Christian and Rainey. That's all I can tell you."

Then Stan Parker exploded: "Tell how you come close enough to Silver to see him without being seen – either by him or that witch wolf that he has along with him?"

"They saw me," said Derry, slowly recounting the facts, reassuring himself of their truth. "They had me roped and tied. Taxi wanted to put an end to me, but Silver seemed to think that I might be a straight shooter – and he turned me loose! Does that sound possible to you?"

"They had you – and they turned you loose?" exclaimed Parker.

He fell into a silence, staring at Derry through the moonlight.

"Christian – he'll want to know about that!" said Parker. "Come along. We got to make tracks. Make it fast. Over the hills yonder, we get a change of horses!"

Over the hill was a long run of second-growth forest, through which they sped at a hard gallop until, in the hollow of the valley, Parker drew rein and whistled through his fingers, a long, trailing screech of high tension. It was instantly answered, so quickly and from such a distance that the second sound seemed an echo. Toward it they rode and found a man with a cluster of three horses, one of them saddled.

"That you, Stan?" he called, while they were still a little way off.

"Here!" shouted Parker. Then, to Tom Derry: "You take the grey. I take the chestnut. Make a fast change, because we've got to burn up the ground. Christian wants us by sun-up, and there's a way to go."

They swung to the ground, pulled off the saddles, jumped them on to the backs of the waiting mustangs.

He who held the animals said: "Who's this, Stan?"

"The hombre that done the trick up there at Blue Water," said Stan. "Derry, this here is Pete Markel."

Pete gripped Derry's hand.

"It was a great job," said he. "You've got the range talkin'. It'll keep on talkin' a good many years after you've danced on air, son!"

Parker and Derry mounted. Away they went, with only a farewell wave. But the words of Pete Markel rang with an evil murmur in the brain of Derry still. It seemed to be taken for granted that he would have to hang, in the end, for saving Barry Christian at Blue Water. Or was it something else? Was it merely that he was now in the association of men whose steps went naturally toward the gallows?

As he rushed the grey after Parker, who was showing the way, he had few chances for thought, but those moments were given to Markel's words, and to the memories of Jim Silver.

Two good men can both be wrong about a given subject. He stuck to that conclusion, finally. About Buck Rainey he would admit no doubts. About Jim Silver he found himself even more assured. Those two men must be straight. It was merely

164

some entanglement of chance, some diversity of interest which made them enemies. Perhaps Tom Derry could manage to bring them together before the finish of the action.

That was the thought that still was pleasant in his mind when, in the pink of the morning, he rode with Stan Parker through a high pass that brought them into one of those small, flat-bottomed mountain valleys that seem certainly the work of glacial ploughs. He had expected to find Christian and Buck Rainey. Instead, he found a whole encampment, of men and horses and dogs, and yonder were women cooking over open fires, and here were children playing or running errands, and farther away spilled a flood of a hundred or more fat-sided cattle.

They were the Cary clan!

"What's happened? What are they doing here?" asked Derry.

"You don't know what's happened to the Cary outfit? Well, you been in the saddle the last few days. What happened was that the Blue Water business was too much for a lot of the gents of that town. They got together, made the sheriff swear 'em in for deputies, and went up to Cary Valley with

165

Walt Milton leadin' 'em. There was a fair-sized scrap. But the Cary gang managed to hold back the Blue Water army long enough for them to hustle their children and their women out of the valley. A few Cary men dropped. So did a few of the boys from Blue Water. That made the posse so mad – to miss rounding up the whole Cary gang, I mean – that the first thing they did was to set fire to the grass in the valley. The flames ran to the house and burned it flat. Half the cattle was burned to death. A scatterin' of 'em came away with the Carys. And the rest were stole, I guess.

"They say that Cary Valley is as flat and bare as your hand, right now. Maybe the Cary's won't be any too happy to see you, old son. I mean, you're the one that led 'em into the fracas at Blue Water, after all. But they've had to throw in with Barry Christian now. The Cary men are mad as hornets and want a lot of action. Folks say that even their land title to the valley is no good at all, and that anybody who wants to can go in and file claims on it. I don't know about that, but I do know that the whole clan ain't got a house to its name. And that throws 'em into the hands of Christian. He can use 'em for steel to cut steel, I guess."

166

As Parker talked like this, they approached the scattered scene of the camp. And what Tom Derry spotted first of all was a broad-branched tree beside the creek, and under that tree the glistening bald head of Old Man Cary. Maria was beside him, cooking over a handful of fire.

Keen eyes had marked Tom Derry as soon as he came close. A general outcry rose, chiefly from the voices of women. The men stood back, watchful, dangerous. But the women were angry. An old hag whose face and body had been roughened and hammered by time and labour into the outlines of a man, ran at Derry and shook her fist in his face. She pranced backward as his horse went on, and she howled at him as she retreated:

"You're him that brought the bad luck to Cary Valley! A curse on your wide mug. A curse on your eyes and heart!"

She turned and brandished her hands at the others.

"Ain't there men here? Ain't there a Cary worth calling a man who'll take hold on him? If there ain't there's women to handle him!"

But there were men, too. They came not rapidly, but steadily.

167

"Get out of here, Derry, if you've got a brain in your head!" advised Stan Parker. Then, as he saw that retreat was cut off by the closing circle of grim faces, he added:

"Well, you got a good pair of hands, I seem to recollect. Why not use 'em?"

And his broad face twisted with a grin of perfect malice.

It seemed to Tom Derry that he had been purposely led into a nest of wasps where he would be stung to death. He stared around him at the big Cary men. They were all armed. Something brightly expectant in their eyes told him that they were prepared to use their guns the instant he turned and tried to escape. There was nothing for it except to sit still in the saddle and argue with them.

He picked out the shaggy black face of big Dean Cary — big even among those giants.

"You fellows know," said Derry, "that I brought you hard cash to make a bargain. You closed for the deal and then you put it through. You got your money and you delivered the right man. After that, you've had some bad luck. Can you blame that on me?"

"Men, are you goin' to stand around and

168

listen to the coyote yap?" screamed the old hag.

Big Dean Cary gripped the reins of the grey gelding.

"Get down!" he said to Derry. "Get down – and we'll do some talkin' face to face. Get down, or maybe we'll pull you down!"

All the other men closed suddenly in around Derry with the hate blazing in their eyes, their hands ready for action.

Maria slid through the crowd.

"Back up, all of you," she said. "The old man wants to talk to him."

"The gal's talkin' like a fool!" shouted the old woman who had roused the clan. "She wants a man and she's come to get him. Bash her in the face. Shut her fool mouth and grab Tom Derry for yourselves! I can tell you some way to treat him!"

"Get out of the way," commanded Dean Cary to the girl.

She did not shrink. Without so much as a glance at Derry, she stepped to the head of his horse and turned on the others, her hands resting on her hips as she faced them.

"If the lot of you think that you have brains to finish without the old man, go ahead and kick him in the face now," she told them. "He sent me to get Derry. I don't know why, but I've come for him. Dean Cary, are you the one that's slapping the old man in the face?"

She pointed a sudden finger at Dean, who stepped back a little and growled:

"How do I know it's the old man who wants him?"

"Did I ever bring you a lie from him before?" asked the girl.

"Leave him go to the old man," said another stalwart. "That don't mean that he's out and away from us. Take him off his hoss so's he can't make no sudden jump – and leave him go and see the old man."

That advice was taken. Powerful hands jerked Derry suddenly out of the saddle and planted him on his feet. A corridor opened through the angry crowd, and down it walked the girl, careless of the fierce faces to either side of her. Tom Derry followed her beyond the throng and to the broad-branched tree under which the old man was seated.

"Well, doggone me," said the old man. "You went and got your man, did you? What's come over the Cary men? Are they gone and turned to milk and water? I reckoned before this here that I'd hear him screechin' like a rabbit with the teeth of the greyhound sunk in it."

"I told 'em that you wanted to see him," said Maria.

"That *I* wanted to see him? I don't want to see him nowhere but dead," said the old man. "I'll tell the boys different!"

And he tilted back his head and opened his wide slit of a mouth to call to the men.

"You yell for the boys," said Maria, "and they'll come and rip him to bits. But here's the only useful man you know outside of Cary Valley, and why d'you want to chew him up so small?"

"Why?" said the old man angrily. "Ain't it him that brought us bad luck? Didn't we have house and land and cows before he come? And look at us now!"

"He didn't drive you out of the valley. The Blue Water men did it," answered the girl. "Might be that Tom could get you back inside again, if you want!"

"Might be? Might not be!" snarled the old man. "You talk like too much of a fool, M'ria."

"Who are you hooked to now, then?" asked the girl.

"To Barry Christian, and you know it."

"Barry Christian's the man that you burned your fingers for. It's for him that the house went up in smoke, and the year's grass along with it, and mighty near all the cattle. *This* isn't Barry. If you want to man-handle anybody, get your grips on Christian."

"He's the goose that lays the golden eggs for us now, M'ria."

"He makes the promises, and you're fool enough to eat 'em," she answered.

"Set down, Tom. Set down, M'ria," said the old man. "Doggone me if it don't stir me up, when I hear the girl talk like this. It pretty nigh chokes me, but afterwards it kind of gives me an appetite."

"I'm busy with breakfast. You two go ahead and yammer together," said the girl. "See what you can come to before the Blue Water men come right down on us again!"

"Ay," muttered the old man. "Have you seen any of 'em headed up this way? "Have you seen anything, Tom?"

"How am I talking to you?" asked Derry pointedly.

"Why," said the old man, "you might as well talk as a friend. I was pretty nigh forgettin' that I shook hands with you once."

"The Blue Water men won't bother you again," said Tom Derry. "You got Christian away from them, but they turned you out of your valley. You broke the law, but so did they. They'll be glad enough to let sleeping dogs lie, I suppose."

"You think so?"

"That's what I guess."

"Maybe you're right. And there's other places than the old valley where we can settle down again. There's more than one Promised Land in this part of the world. Though I reckon I'm maybe goin' to see it but never get into it. Howsomever, we need harsh cash to get more cattle and other things, before we try to set up a new home. And where can we get the cash except from Christian? That's why we're in his hands."

The logic of this was too simple and too clear to be denied. The old man began to load his pipe, wagging his head a little in what seemed to be troubled thought.

"And what'll he use the boys for?" asked Maria suddenly.

She picked a coal from her fire with such swift dexterity that the tips of her rapid fingers were not scorched, and laid the fire on the tobacco in the old man's pipe.

"He'll use the boys for one of his own

crooked schemes," she went on, "and that'll get the law on us harder than ever. Grandpa, you're losin' your wits. There ain't a man in the family that dares to give you advice. Take some from Tom Derry and see how it tastes."

"Him?" said the old man. "How would he be givin' me advice?"

"What else did he come up here for, and risk his bones among your wild men?" said the girl boldly. "Because he had an idea that was worth talkin' about!"

She turned to Tom Derry, who was rather stunned. Then he saw the girl's lips say soundlessly:

"Ask for time!"

"I've got an idea," said Derry in answer, "but I'm not going to spring it at once. I mean to do you good if I can. But why," he continued the words flowing more freely as he embarked on his talk, "but why should I lift a hand or scratch out an idea for you until I make perfectly sure that the Cary outfit is friends with me?"

"There's some sense in that," said the old man, "but what would budge you in the first place to do anything for us?"

"Because I haven't finished paying a price," said Derry.

"A price for what?"

"For the girl, there," said Derry.

The old man chuckled, but his husky laughter did not last very long.

He said: "Some men'll do things for women that they wouldn't have in their heads without 'em, and maybe you've got something up your sleeve for us. M'ria, call in Dean and a couple of the older boys."

She called them in, with her high-piping voice. A semi-circle of half a dozen middle-aged men, including Dean Cary, gathered in front of the old man.

"Boys," he said, "I wanta tell you that this here Tom Derry is a friend of mine, I guess. Maybe he's a friend of all of us. He's goin' to do us some good before we get into a bad pinch. Leave him come and go, but never you leave him come and go except where your guns can point and carry. And on foot is the best way for him to travel. But treat him good. I ain't pleased with everything we been layin' out. The only thing we got in mind is to work for Christian. And you know doggone well that whatever we do for Christian is sure to be crooked, and whatever's crooked brings the law on our heels. And I'm too old to run away from trouble."

175

18

On The Trail

There was enough in that speech to make the Carys scowl, but the control of the old man was still powerful over them. They listened in silence and then drew back. And Tom Derry remained rather dizzy and bewildered by what had happened. He had come close to as horrible a death as a man could think of, he knew, and the girl had saved him from this. But almost more than the danger he had gone through, was the feeling that Christian once and for all had been damned. The old man had said, and it had not been denied, that whatever they were asked to do for Christian was bound to be crooked. If that were true, then Rainey had lied to him about the character of his friend. That saving of Christian at Blue Water had been actually a crime against more than the letter of the law.

And still Derry clung to his old belief in Rainey, like a bulldog to a fighting hold.

176

He would not give up his faith. Somehow the thing would be explained.

He had breakfast in a thick silence with the old man and Maria. At the edge of the creek he got out soap and a razor and shaved. Immediately after that, the journey started.

The Cary clan divided. The women and children and a number of injured or sick men remained behind. In the other party there were seventeen youths or men in the prime of life who were to take the trail. Tom Derry was to go with them. The old man would travel with the outfit and to take care of him there was Maria.

The farewell was very brief, very stern. It seemed to Derry that there was hardly a trace of human emotion in the voices of the clansmen, but when they were at a little distance, he looked back and saw that the mothers were holding up their smaller children to catch the last look at their fathers.

There were plenty of horses, but Derry, according to the will of the old man, had to go on foot. However, the way was very mountainous, and his long powerful legs kept him up with the riders easily enough. He was not very closely guarded. That is to say, men were not constantly at his side. But he knew that their glances were on him and he also knew that every one of the Cary men wanted only a fair excuse to put a bullet into him. The least movement on his part out of line would bring an accurate volley, he was sure.

And the old man headed the advance through the mountains! He sat his saddle with as straight a back as any of the youths, and though he did not ride at more than a walk, and though it was a mule instead of a horse that carried him, still he was plainly the overlord and brains of the outfit. A peculiar grim respect for him was still growing up in the mind of Tom Derry.

He found big Stan Parker in the line of riders and walked for a moment at his side.

"I thought you was gone, sure enough, when they closed in on you. The gal saved your hide, brother," said Parker.

"What was in Christian's head when he sent me up here with you?" asked Derry. "Didn't he know that the Carys were likely to lift my scalp?"

"I don't know what was in Christian's head, and why should I give a damn what happens to you?" asked Stan Parker frankly.

Derry regarded him calmly, and talked no more.

Afterwards, he had a chance to walk near the dancing mustang of "Molly" Cary. Generally she was close to the old man, but the narrowness of a defile had forced her back to a little distance, and there was room for Derry to walk beside her.

"Where are we headed, Molly?" he asked.

"For Barry Christian," she answered.

"Christian? I thought the old man didn't want to deal with him?"

"He don't. But he's made a deal with Christian, and now he's going to carry through his part of the game, unless something better shows up in the meantime. Use your brain, Tom. Try to find a way these fellows can be used."

"In a circus, fighting tigers with their bare hands," suggested Derry.

She did not smile. "You use your head better than that, and maybe you'll save the scalp on top of it," she said. "There's nothing between you and murder except the word of the old man, and that may peg out any time. He's able to change his mind; you've noticed that."

"I've noticed that," agreed Derry.

"What's the deal with Christian?"

She shook her head.

"I'm fond of you, Tom," she admitted, "but I'm not fool enough to trust you with everything, I know. Whatever becomes of me, I'm a Cary, first, last, and all the time."

And she found a chance to urge her pony away from him, while she rode up to regain her place beside the old man.

It was nearly noon of that day, and still the old man was sitting stiff and straight in his saddle, when two horsemen came out of a draw at the side of a wide gulch, two men on splendid horses, who waved their hands as they galloped in.

"Christian!" Derry heard the rider behind him say.

The whole line closed up until Derry could see that it was in fact Barry Christian and Buck Rainey beside him. At the sight of Buck, a vast burden rolled from Derry's heart. He felt that he was breathing easily and deeply again for the first time in days.

He hurried toward Buck as that tall fellow dismounted, the leg which had been wounded sinking a trifle under his weight as he reached the ground. All about there was a general dismounting as Derry got to

Rainey and gripped his hand.

"The devil's to pay," said Tom Derry. "The Carys are out for my scalp. They nearly lifted it this morning. You and Barry had better talk to them, Buck."

"Of course," said Rainey. "Of course, of course!"

He waved, and nodded, and moved into the thick of the talking men.

The old man sat on a rock while Maria Cary made a shade over him with a wide straw sombrero of Mexican make. And before him stood Christian, saying:

"Before we get any farther, we'd better talk about my friend yonder, Tom Derry. Tom, come over here, will you? Now then, tell me what's happened since you started off on my horse."

"Things went all right till the second day," said Derry. "And then I spotted a grey wolf sneaking along behind me. The thing faded out in the brush. That evening, I saw it again. And that night, on the hill over Little Rock, Jim Silver and Taxi jumped me and tied me. The wolf had been Silver's."

"Hadn't you brains enough to guess that?" asked Christian coldly.

The question startled Tom Derry, but he went on:

"I thought Taxi would put an end to me. But Silver seemed to think I might be straight. Anyway, he turned me loose. I got on the black horse and started——"

"Why lie to me?" demanded Christian sternly. "You made a dicker with Jim Silver. He wants a trail laid that will take him up to us. He knew that you'd come this way. He hired you to double-cross us and leave sign that he and his wolf could follow. You cur, you've been a traitor to us. And you're fool enough to think that we won't see through any of your crooked ways?"

19

Thrown To The Dogs

At the pale, handsome face of Barry Christian, Derry could not look. He stared, instead, toward Buck Rainey, as though he might be able to find in the face of his friend some explanation of the strange words of the other. But the horse of Buck Rainey – that same gentle-mannered Nell – became at this moment strangely restive and started dancing and prancing in such a way that Buck Rainey did not seem to be aware of any words that had been spoken. Instead, he was carried to a little distance, quite out of earshot, and had to dismount to begin soothing the frightened horse.

This was almost stranger than anything that Derry had heard from Christian.

The husky, harsh voice of the old man brought him back to his senses.

"If this here's no more'n a rat, then why shouldn't he be treated like a rat?"

"There's no reason in the world," said

183

Christian. "I'm through with him. I wash my hands of him. If you want to waste time on him, Cary, you can do as you please. The sneak is trying to bring Jim Silver on our trail. And if you want trouble of *that* sort, you're welcome to it."

He added: "Come over here, and we'll talk things through. I've a lot to tell you."

With that, he drew the old man aside. Derry, looking wildly about him, saw the savage, the mocking faces of the Carys. He could not hate them, any more than a helpless man could hate wild Indians. He could simply understand the lives they had led and the danger to which their training exposed him now. There was only one face that might hold kindness for him, and that was "Molly" Cary's. He remembered how lightly he had proposed to return to the valley for her one day, and take her away to be his wife – when she had grown up!

Well, she might still be more girl than woman, but she was his main hope for life in this affair. He could not tell what was in her mind now, for her face was impassive. The sun flashed on her as on a dark bronze, she was so stained by many coats of shadowy copper. She had the two long braids of her hair tied around under her chin. She wore a deer-skin jacket that left her round arms bare to the shoulder. She was as unwearied, as straight-backed in the saddle as any of the Cary men. And from a distance she drifted her glance over Derry and the rest just as though he were a most undistinguished feature in the landscape.

Big Dean Cary said calmly: "This is the man that ran us out of the valley and made beggars of us. Anybody got ideas about what we should do to him?"

A young fellow who had dismounted took a long black-snake whip from his neck, around which it was draped. He popped it loudly in the air.

"There's a tree to tie him to, and here something that'll open him up, fast enough. When we see the colour of his blood, we'll know better then!"

"Yeah! Chuck!" shouted three or four voices at once. "Cut him up and see if he stands it as good as a mule!"

They hauled Derry straightway to the tree. They tied his hands and his feet about the trunk and ripped the shirt from his back. Then they cried:

"Now, Chuck, let her go!"

"Lemme see the red the first crack, or *I'll* try the whip."

"Make him holler the first whack or you ain't no good, Chuck!"

"Give it to him, boy!"

The voice of Chuck answered: "Leave him hear this bird sing first, will you? Even a rattler gives a warnin' before it bites, and I'll warn him a little."

Straightway the long lash hummed about the ears of Derry rapidly. Then it popped, and he started as though a gun had exploded a bullet into his flesh.

There was a yell of delight at this sign of fear.

"Take it!" shouted Chuck, and sent the lash home on the bare back of Derry. The thing cut like a sword. The numbing pain of it rushed to his feet, and up into his brain, and worked wildly in the muscles of his throat. But he keep his teeth locked in the good, bulldog grip. His eyes were partly veiled, and through the lids he was able to see his "Molly" Cary sitting calmly on her horse, surveying the scene with folded arms.

That was the truth about her then. She was simply a white-skinned Indian. Ay, not so white-skinned, at that!

"Go get the red, Chuck! That's the boy. You'll have him hollerin' the next pop. Lay

186

it into him!"

The whip fell again. He felt the blow like a hammer-stroke, and there was also a drawing, burning cut that went through the skin.

He locked his jaws harder. He closed his eyes altogether and composed his face, for several of the men had hurried around to study him from the front and read his agonies rather in his face than in the bloody welts that were being painted across his back.

"He kind of bears up pretty good!" he heard one of them mutter. "But Chuck'll wear him down if he has to lay the bones bare!"

Of course, they would whip the flesh from his bones. He would be dead by that time from the loss of blood. A merciful God would let him faint before the agony had lasted that long!

Now Chuck made play with the humming whip about his ears, skillfully fanning the flesh without touching it. At last came a third stroke more terrible than the others by far. This time he could feel the lash, as he thought, sink deep in his body, and a hot flow of blood followed the blow.

"Hi, Chuck! That's openin' him up!"

"He's as soft as butter," said Chuck. "I can cut him near right in two," he went on, panting and happy.

Then several voices shouted in unison: "Get away from there, M'ria! What you mean, you fool girl?"

"I'm here, Tom," said the girl calmly, her voice just at his ear. "If they carve you up it'll have to be through me."

She added to the angry men loudly: "What a lot of cheap hounds you are! Here's a gent that plays a game for Barry Christian, and gets Christian out of jail by getting *us* into the fight. And then Christian turns him down flat. You know why? Because he's too straight for that crook to use any more! Christian gives his horse to Tom Derry so's Tom can draw Silver on to the wrong trail. And Silver does catch up with Tom and grabs him – but two white men can always agree together, and Silver lets him go. There's a heart in Silver. The whole world knows that he ain't any starved coyote.

"He lets Tom go, and Tom gets up to us, where Stan Parker brings him; and then when we meet up with Christian, Christian tells us to do what we please, because he knows that you'll please to cut him to bits. Why? Just because Christian is through with him! That's why. Because Christian thinks that maybe Silver will be able to follow the trail, after all, Christian's thrown him to the dogs – and you're the dogs! I sort of feel lifted up when I look at you. I despise you! There ain't a man of you would fight Tom Derry with his bare hands – but you'll play the pack of dogs to sink your teeth in him all at once!''

They were yipping and yelling with their fury, by this time.

Chuck cried: "Stand away from him, M'ria, or I'll flog you away!"

"I won't budge," said the girl.

"Whip her off!" thundered the larger voice of Dean Cary.

The whip sang. The blow fell – but not on Tom Derry. It cracked again, loudly, and again, on other flesh than his, and gradually his dulled brain could realize through the shouting of the men.

"Give it to her ag'in, Chuck! That'll take the jacket off of her!"

"Hi! There she got it in the face! She's always been too good for us. We'll flog her into a corner. Give it to her ag'in!"

"Yip! That's a good one!"

"Molly," cried Tom Derry, over his shoulder, "get out of it. You can't stop them. I'll take what's coming!"

"I don't even feel it – I'll never budge from here!" she answered.

"Yank her away, some of you!" shouted the voice of Chuck. "Leave me have a go at Derry before my arm gives out on me, will you?"

"Come on, boys," called one man.

Then the girl called out: "If you rush me, I'll blast some of you into the right country – the place you're bound to go. I'll send you there first."

"Put up that gun, M'ria, you young fool!" yelled one.

"Look out – she's goin' to shoot! Back up!"

"M'ria, you'll catch hell, for this. Chuck, knock the doggone gun out of her hand!"

"Get behind her, boys. We'll pull her down. I never seen such a fool for a girl."

The gutteral cry of the old man came out of the distance like a blessing to the ears of Derry.

"What you-all doin' there with M'ria? M'ria, come on up here. Where'd you put my wallet, doggone you?"

She stood back by Tom Derry and
190

slashed the ropes that tied him. He saw, as he turned, how the lash had raised two great welts across her left upper arm. And it had slashed the flesh of her left cheek, also. There was a thin, crimson knife cut, with a purple margin on either side of it.

Derry went mad.

"Give me that gun!" he groaned.

She struck his reaching hand down.

"Don't be a fool. Want them to eat you alive?" she asked.

They swarmed up close. They were savage with eagerness.

"Get back from him, Maria," commanded Dean Cary, "or we'll give you something more to think about!"

"If you edge an inch closer, Dean," said the girl, "I'll blow the face out from between those whiskers of yours. You too, Pete! Chuck, you better go back to the women folks. I'll be even with you for what you've done."

But Derry, his hands gripped into fists, waited for the sudden flooding forward that would be the end of him. Then the voice of the old man called again:

"What you doin' down there? Doggone you brats, you're goin' to hear from me. I'll warm up the hides of some of you if you

191

don't clear away from M'ria. M'ria! Oh, M'ria! Come here, you worthless fool girl, you!"

And that band of stalwarts gave way as though the strength of the voice had cleft a path through them. The girl gripped Derry by the wrist.

"Come along with me!" she commanded. "Walk close. Now, mind you, if there's a hand laid on him, I'm going to start sinking lead into the nearest men. I don't care who I hit. I'd like to butcher the lot of you. You're not Carys. You're only carrion crows. Keep back and give us room!"

They gave room. Many a hand, crooked of fingers with eagerness to grasp at Tom Derry, shrunk away from him. They cursed in savage volleying of oaths. But no grip seized him, and he was led by the hand, like a child, straight up to the place where the old man, Christian, and Buck Rainey were together under a tree.

"Here," said the old man, "what you been spoilin' the fun of the boys for, M'ria? I never seen such a gal! Find me that wallet. Where you put it? There ain't nothin' like a woman for puttin' away things where a gent won't ever find them!"

192

"You're doddering in the brain," she told him, "or you'd have sense enough to look in that left saddlebag. Here you are."

Tom Derry regarded her not. He did not look at Christian, either, except to notice a singular small smile of pleasure that curled the lip of the big man, as he saw the blood on Derry. It was toward Buck Rainey that Derry looked, mining deeply into that man in search for the golden ore of true friendship which must, surely, be hidden away somewhere under the surface. But all that he gained was a sudden shrug of the shoulders and a helpless gesture of resignation, as though Rainey were saying: "You see how things are?"

Ay, but for a friend? There is a code written down somewhere and copied into the hearts of all good men and bad, that friendship must be sacred, and Buck Rainey had allowed his friend to be flogged like a dog at a post. He had not lifted his voice. He had not even raised his hand.

A sudden sickness almost made Derry stagger. He looked down at the ground, breathing hard.

"Here's the paper. Here's the pen. Steady your hand, now. Now you can write," the girl was saying.

"By the jumpin' thunder, M'ria," said the old man, "if you ain't useful, I dunno what is. There, Barry. There's my name wrote out on the thing for you. Mind you take care of it. Look here, M'ria. Who put a whip on to you, I wanta know? I'm goin' to have the hide off his back that – "

"Never mind that. That's my business," said the girl, while Derry listened in amazement. "But d'you want to do something real for me?"

"Hey – of course I do. What would it be, honey?"

"Give me your hand on it?"

"Drat your eyes," said the old man calmly, "now what low trick are you up to, M'ria?"

"D'you give me your hand on it?"

"Well, and here's my hand, too. Fool that I am!" said he.

She grasped that lean claw and shook it.

"I want this man," she said.

"What? Derry? You can't have him. He belongs to Barry Christian."

"What price did Barry Christian pay for him?" she asked.

She turned to Christian. "Except for dirty treachery, what did you ever do to get this man that saved your life, Christian?"

It seemed to Derry that nothing could upset the vast self-possession of this man, but strange to say, he actually lost colour now.

"Keep your females in hand, Cary!" he demanded furiously.

"Did she touch you as deep as that?" asked the old man with a mildly pleased curiosity. "Well, well, well! I guess you can have him, honey. But mind you one thing – he don't get away from the rest of 'em. He's got to stay close with the rest of us, day and night. We can't risk havin' him drop out to mark the way for that devil Jim Silver. Do you understand that?"

"Ay, I understand," she said.

She turned and looked over Tom Derry with a calm eye of possession.

"Lie down on your face," she commanded. "I'm going to fix up them cuts on your back so's you won't ever know that a whip hit you!"

20

The Fight

A home-made salve took the fire out of the whip cuts. The broad, soft bandage eased the ache of the wounds. And still, when the work was ended, and a thin strip of plaster covered the cut on the girl's face, the old man was peering at the designs which Barry Christian drew in the dust, and the soft voice of Christian went on and on, persuading, opening the barrier of the old man's resistance to new ideas.

"The deer-skin may have kept the lash from cutting your body, Molly," said Derry to the girl, after he had huddled into his shirt again, "but there's the welts that whip made."

"I don't mind 'em!" she told him gravely. "They ache a bit and they burn a bit, but that's all right. It keep me thinking about things. And I want to think about them. I want to think about Chuck – and Dean Cary – and some of the others – and about you, Tom."

She had a way of looking at him with no tenderness in her eye, gravely, sombrely, as she had looked at him when she sat on the horse with her arms folded, watching the whip fall on his back. He had to remember that that had been the very instant when she was about to fling herself into the midst of trouble for his sake. Perhaps he would never understand her completely, but complete understanding was unnecessary. There were enough discovered regions of her nature, savage or civilized, to fill his mind. He would only wonder at her, and glory in her.

"There's Dean talking to the old man now," she said. "He's making more trouble. But one of these days he'll have trouble enough to keep him the rest of his days, maybe. I'll think that over, too. I tell you what, Tom, I wouldn't be without the feel of the whip. It's on my body now. And when it heals, it'll still be burning and aching inside my head. Listen! You can hear him. The old man is pretending to be hard of hearing.

The big voice of Dean, in fact, came clearly to Derry, in spite of the distance.

"There's an old rule, and you made it,"

Dean was saying. "No Cary woman goes out to a man until he's paid enough for her to suit you and the rest, or until he's fought for her."

"Ay, that's a rule, and a good rule," said the old man. "What's the Cary that wants the gal, though?"

"There's Hugh Cary willing to fight for her," said Dean.

"Ain't Derry been beat enough for one day to suit you?"

"He ought to be hanging on that tree, dead, to suit most of us," said Dean Cary. "He's the cause of all our troubles. But we'll stay right to the point. You give Derry to the girl. That's all right – if you do it inside the rules. But Derry can't have her without fighting for her, and she can't have him. There's a rule in that, I guess."

"I'm tired of the whole mess," said the old man. "I kind of thought that she was goin' with him up there in the valley. You was willing enough to that when he'd paid in money. And then he wouldn't have her, and she come back – and everything got all tangled up. Gals and boys are fools, I say. There ain't any way of makin' 'em out. But if there's gotta be a fight, let it happen. I wouldn't care. Call up Derry, and call up

Hugh, and they fight the way the stranger wants. That's always the rule, I guess."

Dean Cary turned away with a happy face and hurried toward the place where the rest of the clan sprawled in the shade.

"Do you hear, Tom?" said the girl. "Are you dead on your feet? Are you shaky from the whip? Can you fight?"

"Ay," he said, "I can fight. Gun or knife or hands."

She picked up one of his hands with both of hers and spread the fingers.

"We're raised with guns and knives. Hands will have to to do for you, Tom. You've got a pair of hands. But, oh, Hugh Cary's a big man! He's the biggest man that ever walked in the valley, I guess. Look at him getting up!"

It seemed to Tom Derry, staring, that the great hulk would never stop rising. That was Hugh Cary who threw his hat on the ground, and laughed. Inches and inches over six feet, and bulking great in proportion, he looked strong enough to pull against a horse. He was in the very height and prime of life. He was clean-shaven. He had the heavy brow and the craggy jaw of a born battler. And he had the step of a young horse full of mettle,

199

dauntless, unbeaten.

And sud'denly Tom Derry thought of his own weight, his own gaunt body.

Well, he had a set of hitting muscles. He might surprise them, after all.

"You can get out of it," said the girl. "Say no – say you don't want me. That's all you need to say. No, don't throw your head. I'd understand. What's the good of a useless fight? Why get yourself all bashed up for nothing?"

Hugh Cary walked straight up to Derry and towered over him. The rest of the clan followed on rapidly, grinning at one another. One of the men was patting the wider shoulder of Hugh Cary in admiration.

"You want M'ria, do you?" said Hugh Cary to Tom. "But how do you want her? Knife or gun or club or hands, or anyway you say, I'm your man! I'm goin' to fight for you, M'ria," he added to the girl, "whether you want me to or not. I got an idea that I could tame you!"

"You've picked your time," said the girl. "When he's walked half the day. When the blood's been let out of his body. That's the time to pick a man for a fight, and you well know it. But one day *I* may have to show you that there's something more than size that counts. And well I'd like the chance to do the showing!"

"Take off your gun, in case you'd get careless," said Tom Derry. "It'll be hands, Hugh."

"Hands?" said Hugh Cary, his eyebrows lifting in amazement. "Hands, you runt?" he added, stepping closer to measure his bulk against Derry.

"Ay, hands, you clumsy fool," answered Derry calmly.

He looked about him at the ground. There were only moccasins on the feet of Hugh Cary. They would grip the smooth of the rock well, so Tom Derry dragged off his boots, and put his bare feet on the hot stone. If the skin cut on rough places here and there – well, that was a small thing.

Hugh had tossed off his coat, laughing. His gun belt he shed, and threw a big bowie knife after it.

"How does the betting go, boys?" he asked.

"Get your hip and thigh hold, Hughie," said one cheerful fellow, in the midst of the laughter, "and slam him up against the rock, and he'll squash just like a rotten tomato."

"Yeah, and I'll get my hands on him," said Hugh Cary. "Are you ready, runt?"

"I'm ready," said Derry.

"Tom," said the girl suddenly, "will you kiss me?"

He leaned over her till his face was close. She closed her eyes and waited. He straightened, without touching her.

"Ay, afterwards," said Derry. "When I've earned the right."

He spun about to face Hugh Cary. It was not going to be easy. That vast bulk, even untaught in boxing and wrestling, would be hard to handle, but Hugh Cary stood with a high guard, with the perfect balance of a man who knows thoroughly well how to take care of himself with his fists.

He seemed a mighty picture of what a fighter ought to be. But then the old savour of battles in the past rushed up into the mind of Tom Darry. He had to run away for fear of what his hands might do. And now battle was demanded of him as a right! He thought of forecastle and bunkhouse, of land and sea, and a hundred faces grinning at him in the battle rage.

Fine pictures are not the beginning and the end-all in a fight, so Derry tried an old ruse. He walked in high on his toes, his guard low. He saw the flexion of arm and body. He saw the blow shoot for his head, and, ducking just under it, he rammed both hands, one after the other, into the soft of Hugh Cary's body.

He hit where the soft should have been, at least, but the man was banded about with india-rubber. The blows rebounded foolishly.

And Derry jumped back as an overhand punch grazed his head.

The Carys were yelling and dancing. Hugh Cary wore a silly smile. The smile went out. He seemed infuriated because he had not ended the battle at the first meeting, and now he charged.

It was no blind rush. It was open-eyed, with a long straight left prodding like a battering-ram to make passage for the charging bulk. Well, body punching would do no good on the rounded barrel of Hugh's chest or against the corrugations of muscle that guarded his stomach.

Tom Derry ducked his head outside that prodding left first, made the little hitch step that throws weight into a punch, and slammed his left with all his might against the point of the chin.

He stepped back, his arm trembling and

half-numbed to the elbow, looking for the stagger of Hugh Cary, looking for the chance to put in the finishing blow with his right.

But the giant turned with a shout of rage and gripped him in open hands.

There is a trick of diving at a man's feet, at a time like that. Derry tried that trick. The shirt ripped off his back, and the skin came off under the cloth, where the fingers of the big man were gripping. But Derry slid out of that dangerous hold and twisted to his feet in time to swerve like a snake away from the next charge.

There was a blackness of despair in his heart. He could hardly hurt the monster with body punching. To batter his jaw seemed little more than to hit a rock.

There was the mouth. There were the eyes. And little, little hope.

But he tried with both hands. Desperation made him stand in close, and as Hugh Cary turned, Derry slashed him with a left and right across the eyes. Then he sprang back and saw the blood go down in two trickles across the face of Hugh Cary.

And better by far than wine to a thirsty man was the sight of that crimson to Derry.

He did not know that a wild cry came out of his own throat. He did not hear the shout of dismay from the Cary clansmen. He only knew that he had made one step toward victory, and he went in like a tiger to draw blood again. It was the overhanging swing, tried and true, and sweet and straight it landed now, full on the right eye of Hugh Cary.

In return, he received a lifting blow that cracked him under the chin and sent him running backward on his heels, with loosened knees.

The image of the monster, coming in hot pursuit, wavered before his eyes; the shouting of the men was like the roar of a distant sea. Then the shrill cry of the girl stabbed through the mists that covered his eyes and cleared them away.

An arm like a walking beam was hurling ruin toward his head. He barely managed to duck under the whir of the blow. He turned, his head clear, his feet light, his knees strong. And now he saw, as Cary turned, what those cutting blows had acomplished.

One of Hugh's eyes was quite closed and puffing. The other was streaked across with crimson. As Cary ran in again to finish his man, Hugh could not help lifting a hand to brush quickly at the blood which was dimming his sight.

It was as though he had pointed out the target, and Derry sprang swiftly in with a blow that landed true again.

Perhaps pain more than shock made Hugh Cary give back with both eyes closed and running blood.

He squared off, but turned away almost at right angles from Derry.

And Tom said: "Your man's not able to see. Do you want me to hit a blind man, you fellows?"

They made no answer. The silence was thick and heavy in which they went to Hugh Cary and led him away as he moaned:

"He had something on his hands. He had something over his knuckles. He tricked me!"

A hand touched that of Derry and lifted it. That was the girl, leaning to stare at the broken flesh across the knuckles, for Derry had split the skin until the bone and gristle showed white underneath.

21

Headed For Gold

When the march began again, it turned and angled straight north through a canyon that led into a broken sea of mountains. In fact, the peaks often had wave shapes, the tall crests curving up and seeming ready to break forward or back. But they were all naked rock, those summits. That was why they shone like water in the afternoon sun.

Even the scenery grew wilder and stranger, and Derry trudged on silently. The sweat sprang constantly on his skin and instantly dried away to a dust of salt in the acrid air. Some of the ravines were tormenting ovens. Others were merciful flumes of shadow through which the waters of coolness poured over the marchers. And always, up there in the lead, the old man and Barry Christian led the way. The strength of Old Man Cary in the saddle was an amazing thing. He could hardly walk without tottering, but in the saddle he was of redoubled strength.

In the heat of the day, he stripped off his shirt. His head was left bare, and that polished scalp always carried a burning highlight. He seemed to be on fire, but he preferred the Indian half-nakedness to clothes of any sort. One could see the wide spring of his shoulders, the gaunt tendons that reached up and down the sides of his withered neck. One could count his ribs like great fingers clasping his skeleton sides. He was death-in-life. But he was up there at the head of his clan, and something told Tom Derry that the old man would die before he relinquished his place. He had been content to loll about when he was still in the valley which he had made the home of his people, but when they were cast out of that residence, he would lead them again until they found means to settle in another place. There was still more strength in his will than in all the rest of his people.

In the meantime, Derry was guarded before and behind. He had expected that the Carys would treat him with more hatred than ever, since his battle with Hugh. Instead, their entire attitude seemed to have undergone a favourable change. And finally Hugh himself, with blood-stained

208

bandages over his face, rode up beside the pedestrian and dismounted, and, and walked with him for a little.

"I'd give you the mustang to ride," said Hugh Cary, "but most of the boys would be agin' it. They're comin' around, but most of 'em would still be agin' it. Doggone me, they want to see how long you can last on foot, like this."

The friendliness underlying this speech amazed Derry, and he stared at his huge companion.

The one battered eye of Hugh that appeared under the edge of the upper bandage squinted back at Derry with something like humour.

"You licked me proper," Hugh declared. "Them that know always lick them that don't know. The old man says that, and the old man can't be wrong. One of these days, maybe you'll teach me how to box. You got an overhand wallop that dropped on me out of nothin' at all. It sure plastered me. It dragged my face all down toward my chin. But it taught me something."

His cheerfulness was immense.

"When you socked me that first couple in the ribs, I thought you was goin' to keep hammerin' at the body. Why didn't you?"

"Because it was like hitting at the staves of a barrel," said Derry, smiling in turn.

"Those punches sprung the staves of the barrel so doggone bad it pretty nigh gave me heart failure," admitted Hugh. "I laughed, but I felt pretty sick. That was what brung my guard down, and you got at my face. My jaw pretty nigh was cracked, the first time you slammed it. But the eyes – you didn't hit nothin' but eyes, after that. I felt like my eyes was each as big as a saucepan. Where'd you learn to box, brother?"

"On a ship," explained Derry. "A fellow taught me. I had to learn or get my head knocked off. And I got my head knocked off a good many times before I learned how to block. After I could block, then I had to learn how to hit. There were only two buttons that rang a bell in the head of that Yankee skipper. One was the point of his chin, and one was the centre of his stomach."

Hugh Cary laughed. Then, growing more sober, he asked: "How come Barry Christian to hate you so much? Because you hooked up with Jim Silver?"

"I didn't hook up with Silver. He had me

– and he let me go. That was all." Then he added, out of the bitterness of his heart: "But I wish that I *had* hooked up with Silver."

"Ay," said Hugh Cary, "I seen him once. I seen him, and Frosty, and Parade. I come over a ridge, and on the next one, toward the sun, there was a deer runnin' lickety-split. You never seen a deer leg it like that one. It was half a mile off, and no good my tryin' at it. And then the deer takes a jump in the air, and drops, and lies still, and I hear the report of a rifle come floatin' up to me soft and easy out of the hollow of the valley, like a trout driftin' up through still water. And I looked down there into the hollow and I seen a golden hoss, and a grey wolf, and a man. I couldn't see the man very good, but by the shape of his head and shoulders, I'd know him again. He looked like he could lift a ton or run faster than a stag. I knew him by the look – and that was Jim Silver. It give me a kind of creeps, seein' him like that. I was glad that he hadn't seen me instead of the deer."

"Why?" asked Derry. "He wouldn't have shot at you, would he?"

"Maybe not," said Cary, "but you might

'a' noticed that the Carys are kind of wild and free and do as they please, no matter what toes they step on. And Jim Silver don't like that sort of thing. He's best pleased by them that keep their own places. Wildness he don't like, and every man that does wrong is kind of a private enemy, for Silver. It ain't no business of his, but he makes it his business. Understand?"

"I begin to understand," said Derry gloomily.

"And no man could stand agin' him," said Hugh Cary, with awe in his voice, "except that lies and meanness is things that Silver don't understand, and that's why Barry Christian is still got two legs to walk on the earth, instead of bein' dead and under the ground. Here comes M'ria driftin' back, and I reckon she wants to talk to you. Be seein' you ag'in, partner."

There was something about this interview that cleared the mind of Derry of many obscurities. It made of Buck Rainey, for one thing, a complete and perfect liar, for Derry remembered every word of Rainey's first description of Silver as the incarnation of evil. It made of Rainey the type of the lying, shifting enemy who managed to exist against Silver by sheer force of trickery, and not of strength.

It made of Silver himself that brightness and greatness at which Derry had been able to guess when he was still in the hands of the strange man.

Then "Molly" Cary was back beside him. She, too, dropped from the saddle to the ground and stepped lightly along with him. The whip welt that ran off the bare of her shoulder under the deer-skin jacket had grown and swollen; it was a bright crimson now. But when Derry asked her about it, she merely smiled. She said not a word. And then she examined him with her eyes, brightly and carefully.

"The whip cuts are stinging you pretty bad, Tom," she remarked, "but as long as they don't make you sick, it's all right. Pain doesn't matter. Not till it makes you sick. What was Hugh saying?"

"Asking me to teach him boxing."

"He's the best of the lot – except the old man. He's more like what the old man must have been."

Derry squinted ahead at the drawn skeleton that was now the old man, but if that frame were stuffed out with young power and sleeked over with young flesh, it might well have been closely similar to the

213

bulk of Hugh.

He asked the girl where they were heading.

"For Wool Creek," she said.

"And for what?"

"Gold," she answered. "Christian has news about a gang of men that went up through the old diggings on Wool Creek. Tenderfeet, mind you! Away up there, to have a vacation and shoot at deer they couldn't hit, and fish for trout they couldn't catch, and then one of them finds an old pan and washed out some mud – and there's gold in the pan! Well, that's the story – and at that the whole crowd went wild, and started washing, and they've been there washing gold for a couple of months, and they've found tons of it."

"Tons?" exclaimed Derry.

"A whole lot of it," she answered. "Enough to load a lot of mules, anyway. They've started coming up Wool Creek, now, to head through the pass and get back to civilization and all be rich, but I guess they'll have to go through without the gold. It'll stick to Christian and Cary fingers!"

She laughed as she said this.

"How does that strike you, Molly?"

"Why, it strikes me good," she

answered, surprised. "Why not?"

"Robbery?" he asked. "That strikes you good, does it?"

"Robbery?" she answered, frowning. "No, you wouldn't rob anyone you know. You wouldn't rob a friend. You'd die first. But robbing strangers – what's wrong with that?"

Derry looked blankly ahead of him, and stumbled over a rock. He was amazed. No matter how long he was with this odd clan, he still was very far from coming to any clear understanding of them. Their habits of living were queer, but their habits of thinking were yet more odd.

"We'll clean 'em out," said the girl, with enthusiasm, "and then the Cary share of it, along with the money the old man got for setting Christian free, will be enough to buy us another valley, somewhere off in the mountains – a bigger and better valley than we had before, somewhere that the winters won't be so cold and freeze so many cows, every now and then. We'll have enough money to stock the new place, too, they say. And you'll move in with the rest of us and settle down with me."

Her eyes shone as she visualized the future.

215

Derry spread out his hands.

"Look, Molly," he said. "I've always lived off the thick of the skin of my hands. I'll keep on living that way. Stolen money may be all right for the Carys, but it's no good for the Derrys."

"You've got some funny ideas," she told him. "I don't like that one."

"Don't you?" asked Derry, setting out his jaw. "I'll tell you a funnier idea than that one, though. When you and I settle down, you won't be a Cary any longer. You'll be a Derry."

"Will I? Well, it sounds about the same."

"It won't be the same, though. The Derrys are straight. They don't live on loot."

She flew into a passion. "What do I care about you and your ideas?" she exclaimed. "Gold was made to be taken, and only fools won't try to get their share. You're too good for the Carys, are you? Then you're too good for me!"

So she whipped into the saddle and rode hastily back to rejoin the old man.

22

The Trap

The latter part of the day's march was along tremendously difficult terrain, labouring up and down the ridge of a high range; and in the evening they came within sound of the voice of falling water and defiled on a broad, flat shoulder of rock with only enough earth on it to support a scattering growth of grass and of shrubbery. Opposite them there was a similar shoulder of rock, with the mountains climbing above it. In between was the cleavage of a narrow gorge through which poured and leaped the thundered waters of Wool Creek.

From these narrows, the valley widened immediately to the north, the mountains sloping gently down from the height on which the Carys were posted. To the south, there were cliffs two or three hundred feet tall. Whoever went down Wool Creek from the south to the north found himself compelled to pass through a very narrow gorge, along a ledge of stone which seemed to have been carved out of the rock on purpose to make a path. Looking down at it from the edge of the dizzy cliff, it seemed to the eye of Derry, in most places, hardly wide enough for a single rider, but perhaps it was more spacious than it seemed.

It was plain that the old man and Christian had hit upon the most logical place for committing the robbery of the gold caravan. The men who were carrying the treasure would have to pass through those narrows – into a trap. If they came by Wool Creek, there was no other way for them to go except on that narrow place.

Here camp was made. A small rivulet of water was of great use for horse and man, but no fire was made. The orders of the old man were strictly against any rise of smoke to betray their position. On jerked meat and parched corn and cold water, the Carys could subsist until they had made sure of their prey. To Derry, the plan seemed flawless, but he wondered at the approach to the place.

He managed to say to Hugh Cary: "Why did we have to wind around through the rocks and the mountains, along the crest, when we might have cut across the hills and

218

got into the upper valley of Wool Creek long ago?"

"We've got Silver on our trail, ain't we?" said Hugh Cary. "Maybe you know that a lot better than I do, but you don't know it better than the old man, and Christian. And we've laid a trail across rocks where the sun will burn up the scent and not even Frosty can follow it. We've laid a trail problem that's taken us a good long while, but we've beat Jim Silver off the trail!" And he laughed triumphantly.

Before darkness came, Derry was tied, and very cleverly. He was allowed to have his hands before him, but around each wrist, fitted snugly, was a bracelet made of many twists of baling wire, big, heavy, soft strands of it which were worked afterward through links of a light chain, and the chain had, in the first place, been passed around the trunk of the only tree of any size that stood on the rock shoulder.

That seemed to fasten him securely enough. Afterward, lookouts were placed on the edge of the northern slope and the southern cliff, and the party was ready to wait for its game.

As the stars came out, Buck Rainey sauntered up to Derry and sat down beside him.

"How does the layout look to you, Tom?" he asked cheerfully.

"For crooks and robbers," answered Derry deliberately, "it looks like a fine job."

"You're not insulting me," replied Rainey. "Whatever you say about crooks and robbers goes with me. I've been one for a good long spell, Tom."

"Let that go!" broke out Derry. "But, ah, man, man, we were friends, and yet you didn't lift a hand to help me!"

There was a silence. Then Tom added: "Seems to me that if I'd seen you under the whips, as I was, I would have tried to do something. I would have tried to say something!"

"It would have been no good," said Rainey. "Barry decided that you had to be blotted out of the picture, just then. I argued with him about it. I told him that you'd do no harm. But he hates Silver so much that he's a little blind on the subject. Couldn't budge him."

"What did he say? What have I ever done to him except save his neck at Blue Water?" demanded Derry.

"You've never did him anything but
220

good," said Rainey, "But that hardly matters. You've been in the hands of Silver, and you've come out of them safe. To Christian's eye that means you're the friend of Silver now. And that means that you're better dead than living. Does that make any sense to you?"

"I understand," said Derry. "Suppose I tell you something, Buck. I've been in Silver's hands. I got away from him – he let me go. And I swear that he didn't make me promise to help him against anyone. He didn't even talk to me against Christian. But when Taxi wanted to do me in, Silver simply said that I could go free, because no honest man would be useful in the long run to Christian."

"Ay, did he say that?" asked Rainey.

"He did."

"Perhaps he's right," agreed Rainey. "Perhaps he could turn you loose blindly and trust you to make trouble for Christian. But even if Silver's no smart trickster, there's something deep about him. No crook in the world would ever have thought that far ahead. If Silver had tried to persuade you to double-cross Christian and me – why, perhaps he would have had to buy you high!"

221

"There's no money in the world to buy me," said Derry.

"No?" murmured Rainey. "How the devil does that come?"

"I'll tell you how. I was crooked once at cards. I got eighteen dollars off a shipmate. When I say I was crooked, I mean I played with that Swede when he was too drunk to have sense. I went and blew in the eighteen dollars on a drunk of my own. But afterward, the thing kept boring into me. I couldn't look the Swede in the face. And when the next pay-off came, I gave him back his eighteen bucks. That taught me that crooked money was worse than nothing to me."

Rainey listened to this explanation with faint exclamations of wonder.

"People are made in two ways, Tom," he said at last, "and you were made in the right way. I was made in the wrong way. That's all there is to it."

"You weren't made wrong," said Derry. "But Christian may keep you wrong. You saved my life — twice. Nobody ever did a better thing. You didn't even know me, but you ate lead to help me in a pinch."

"I don't say I'm all devil," admitted Rainey. "I like you, Tom. I still like you;

I'd do anything I could for you. But Christian——"

His voice fell away.

"What do you get out of Christian?" asked Derry.

"The chance to kick down the old walls and see new chances," said Rainey thoughtfully. "The chance to play for long odds – and win right along. The chance to live as other men can't live. Look at it this way: I knew about those miners on Wool Creek and that they were about to head back for civilization with their loot. A dozen, or fifteen of 'em in all. Tenderfeet, but able to shoot straight enough. Tough and hard from the work they'd been doing. Keen as mustard, the whole lot. I needed help to get their gold. What help? Who could I trust to give me a hand in robbing them without robbing *me* of my share, afterward? Christian! I mortgaged my soul to get a lot of hard cash. I sent word to Stan Parker because I knew I could trust that muttonhead to carry the coin for me. You stepped by chance into Parker's shoes – because you were a good fellow. Sort of romantic, but the best fellow in the world. And so the game worked out, and there's Christian over there, using his brain, working out the deal that's sure to put us all in clover!"

Dimly Tom Derry could follow the workings of the brain of Rainey.

"When the whip was on me, what about that?" he asked finally.

"I made my horse raise a ruction. Then, when the flogging began, I stuffed my fingers in my ears, and only took them out when the girl showed up. She's a queer, pretty devil of a girl, Tom. What are you going to do with her?"

"Marry her, when she's a brace of years older."

"She's coming now," said Rainey. "She's been taking care of the old man. Tough old hombre he is, but he's wax in her hands. I'll leave you alone with her."

As Rainey left, she came up, stood for a moment above Derry, then sank down to the ground beside him.

"Well?" she said.

"Well?" said Derry tersely.

"You still full of fool ideas?" she asked.

"What ideas?"

"That you're better than the Carys?"

"I'm better than any gang of thieves," said Derry.

"Wait a minute," said the girl. "You see

a deer, and you're hungry. Do you shoot the deer?"

"Yes."

"That's stealing the deer's life, isn't it? Then why not see a man with gold and take the gold, if you're strong enough to do it?"

He gaped at her through the darkness.

"Go on and answer me if you can," said the girl.

"All I know is what I feel is right," said Derry.

"All I know is that I like your ugly mug," said the girl. "What's the use of thinking such a lot about right and wrong? Being happy is the main chance. Look at the deer. It's happy on good grass and sweet water. But along comes a man with a gun and turns that deer into venison. The deer was right to be happy as long as it could. The man was right to eat when he could. You can't get behind that, Tom."

"Maybe not," he answered. "It sort of makes my head ache to think of it."

She put her hand on his forehead.

"Ay," she said, "your head's hot. I'll get a cold rag and put it on it."

"No, but keep your hand there. Now look up yonder. See that big yellow star? There's five stars spread out ahead of it.

225

See it?"

"Yes," said the girl.

"I've steered by that star. There was hell blowing at sea, that night. But the sky was clear, and I steered the old ship by Arcturus. Well, old girl, it's like that all the time. Sometimes we get into a blow, and then we want to turn and run with the wind. But it's better to steer for the right things, no matter how small and far away and useless they look. Understand that?"

"I sort of understand," she said.

"There's another thing," he said. "Some men are hellions on shore but good shipmates in a storm. No matter what ideas you got in your head, you're a good shipmate in a storm, Molly."

"Well," she said, after a pause, "what else matters?"

"Nothing much," said Derry.

23

The Gold Caravan

They spent that night and the next morning in freezing cold until the sun rose, and in burning heat thereafter. The girl brought news at noon.

"The old man says that after this job's done, and Silver's surely off the trail, then maybe he can turn you loose," she told Derry. "But are you going to want to be turned loose? There's a lot of the men that feel pretty friendly about you, Tom. Hugh's always got a good word for you. And that's hard on him, because he wants me for his wife, you know. Suppose you stayed on with us! The old man would have you, all right. He'd have you, for my sake."

Derry shook his head stubbornly.

"All there is to it, I've got to live by my own hands and my own head," he told her.

And she went gloomily away.

The sun sloped off into the west, and a kind mountain-top reached up a shadow that blotted away the steady rain of fire, at last. It was just after that, that the northern look-out came hurrying to the rest with word that a dust cloud was travelling slowly up the side of Wool Creek. It might be the gold caravan.

The rest hurried off to look down the valley. And Derry, standing on tiptoe beside his tree, was able to see the cloud of dust turn into a string of little figures, some mounted men, and others pack animals, going ahead at a steady pace.

They halted not half a mile from the entrance to the gorge and rapidly began preparations for the camp. It was the gold caravan! Buck Rainey, using a strong glass, had actually identified some of the men and the animals. And yet, as the jubilation started in the Cary camp, a sudden report from the watcher on the southern cliff checked all rejoicing.

Derry, no matter how he stretched and strained on tiptoe, could not see into the pit of the southern valley below the cliff, but he could take the picture from the words of the Cary men, and from the strained, set face of Barry Christian.

Two riders had come out of the trees and were camping at the edge of the creek, close to the entrance of the gorge on the southern side. Two riders made little difference, or would have made a small difference to the Cary plans, ordinarily. But one of these men was on a big horse that shone like copper in the last sunset light, and with the two riders there was a great skulking monster of a grey wolf.

There was no question about it. Jim Silver and Taxi had managed to guess at the destination of the Cary party without having to follow the complicated trail across the mountain ridges.

There were the two men whom Christian feared most – and almost within hailing distance.

Yet that difference was too far, and the light too uncertain, to suggest snipe shooting. Moreover, the two men were moving back and forth, rarely glimpsed through the brush as they made their camp quickly. Derry saw Christian walk by, with his hand gripping the arm of Buck Rainey.

"If only Silver and Taxi will ride on through the canyon!" groaned Christian.

"Ay," said Rainey, "after we've cleaned up the gold caravan."

"Damn the caravan!" answered Christian. "What's the money compared with the chance of getting that devil off my trail once and for ever?"

Rainey nodded.

"We'll spread out and surround the gold camp and tackle it after moonrise," said Christian. "We'll leave two or three men in the throat of the canyon to stop Silver and Taxi if they should happen to get one of their strange notions and march on after dark. We've still got every chance of taking both bags of game, Buck. Man, man, you've brought me out of trouble into a lot of good luck, I can tell you!"

A score of well-armed and trained fighting men, and separated enemies who did not know of the existence of an ally near at hand – what better chance could Barry Christian have asked for? In fact, it seemed to Tom Derry that the thing was as good as done already. First, they would swallow the gold camp. The noise of the rifles would never stretch through the canyon and warn Silver. Instead, the thundering of the waterfall was sure to muffle and cover that tell-tale sound.

So the darkness thickened over the plateau, and by the starlight Derry saw the preparations go forward. No watch was kept over the southern cliff now, since

Silver's camp was invisible in the darkness below. All the men were gathered along the northern edge of the plateau where the slope ran easily down into the valley.

That was when the girl came back to Derry and stood above him for a long moment. The roaring of the waterfall seemed to be wavering back and forth in the air, now drifting farther, now coming nearer.

"Suppose you were a free man, Tom, what would you do?" she said finally.

"Get into it!" he said. The mere suggestion made his heart leap up till he was almost suffocated.

"How could you get into it?" she asked. "The Carys are there to the north, and you couldn't get through them. There's a cliff to the south, and you're not a bird to fly down to Jim Silver."

"There's a cliff straight down to the river," he said. "but it's not absolutely straight. There are juts and knobs of rocks. I saw one long crevice that a man could get a handhold in and slant down a hundred feet toward the bottom."

"A fly would get dizzy trying to make a climb like that," she reminded him.

"I'm not a fly, but I wouldn't get dizzy."

"Suppose you got to Silver – you might save his neck, but you couldn't possibly help the gold camp."

"Maybe not. But saving Silver would be something."

"What puts you on fire to help him?"

"Why do you ask that, Molly? You know he had me and could have smashed me, but he turned me loose."

She was silent again.

"What sort of a snake would I be," she muttered, "if I turned you loose? You'd never get down the cliff alive. And if you did, I'd be a traitor to my men!"

"Going straight is stronger than blood," said Derry. "And what are people like you and me, compared with a man like Silver?"

"The air tastes as good to me as it does to him," she answered. "The mountains are as free to me as they are to him. Tom, will you give up the thinking about him like a wise man? Or will you carry it all your life with you, if something goes wrong with Jim Silver tonight? Will you hate me every time you look at me?"

"No," said Derry. "I wouldn't hate you. I wouldn't do that. But——"

He paused.

She began to sob, not like a woman, but

like a man, the deep sounds tearing her throat. Then, when she could talk, he could feel the force of will that enabled her to speak steadily again.

"The women are the deer. They run about like little fools. And the men turn 'em into venison. If I turn you loose, you'll be dead before morning. If I don't turn you loose, you'll despise me for being what I am. You'll hate me with your eyes, no matter what you speak with your mouth. Why was I ever born a Cary? But I'd rather be a Cary thief than any other name that's honest. If I set you free, the Carys will turn me out like a dog. If I set you free, you're dead, too."

She threw herself down by him.

"Tom, will you listen?" she asked. "I could make you a happy man and forget all that happens tonight. It's only one night. What can happen in a night to make the rest of your days dark for you? If you're sad a while, I'll pull up the old sun for you like a bucket out of a well. I'll love you till you love me back, and a man and a woman together, they're the only ones that can make happiness. Truer than anything, that's true. Are you hearing me, Tom! Or are you thinking about Jim Silver and the

233

death he's coming to?"

"I'm loving you, Molly," said he, "but I'm breaking my heart because of Jim Silver."

She sat up from him suddenly.

"Ay," she said at last, "what for should I go on talking? I knew you wouldn't be the kind of a rat that a woman could budge by just talking. I've got the clippers to free you, and I'll use 'em now. And ten minutes after, the river'll be eating you! May it eat me, too! May it swaller me!"

She gripped his wrists, pried, a forefinger under the wires to lift them above the flesh, and then clipped rapidly until one hand, then the other, was free.

He stood up, lifting her with him, and she hung loose against him.

"Will you wait a minute?" she asked.

"There's no time for waiting."

"I'll go to the cliff with you, Tom."

"This way," he said. "I marked the place where the crack runs down the wall, if I can get to it."

They came to it. The roar of the river burst up at them in increasing explosions. The humidity of incredibly fine spray filled the air, and he drew the girl back from the edge of the rock for a moment. There was

234

no strength in her. It seemed that she would drop to the ground if his arm left her.

"When you're down, will you light a match?" she begged him. "And if I wait for ten minutes – and see no light——"

"Mind you, Molly," he said with a frightful cold of fear sweeping over him, "whether you see it or not, you won't do any fool thing?"

"What have I done but fool things ever since I found you?" she said. "I've been like a fool boy, ranting around; I haven't been a woman to you. I wish I'd been a woman to you. Then, light or no light, I'd have something more than a – than a damned star in the sky to steer by after you're gone. But go on now, Tom, I'm dying, and I want you gone. I'm going to lie out there on the rock and wait for the sparkle of a match down there. God grant I may see it, or else——"

He kissed her. The fear of what she might do made his lips numb. He dreaded lest that fear should work downward to his heart, and so he left her suddenly and went to the edge of the rock.

He had found the right place, he knew. Below him, though unseen, there was a narrow ledge which he ought to be able to touch with his feet. If he could drop to that, a crevice slanted away to the side and downward. And if he could reach that——

Well, if he failed in getting from one place to another, it might not be many minutes before another and a slighter body than his own hurtled through thin air and into the white water beneath.

24

The Perilous Journey

The ledge which had seemed in reach of his feet, when he should dangle at the full stretch of his arms, was, in fact, still out of touch. He let himself drop, with such a looseness of knees as though he might have to fall fifty feet, and the impact nearly rammed his knees against his chin when he struck. It was well enough that he had fallen like a length of loose rope, for as he spilled over on one side, his arm dangled down into nothingness. The ledge was hardly a foot and a half wide – but he was safely on it.

To get back to the upper ledge was now impossible. He looked up, and the distance seemed immense. The moisture of the air was very palpable. The roaring of the echoes certainly had increased. He had the distinct feeling that the river, a sentient thing, was shouting out a triumph over him. It might have been that even the cliff

237

was shuddering a little from the vibration set up by the waterfall. He would rather think that than believe that he was already trembling.

Down the ledge he worked to the very end of it, and feeling down with an anxious hand, he found what he wanted – the beginning of that crack which he had marked from the top of the rock during the daylight. He swung down to it.

He had gone hand over hand along many ropes during his days at sea, but no rope could have the zigzags and the irregularities of this crack. A rope gave a whole handhold. The crevice was something in which he had to trust to the flat of his hooked fingers.

He could not give his full mind to himself. His preoccupation dealt with Molly Cary at the top of the cliff. Already the moments had spun themselves out a great distance for her, perhaps. The thought of her was like a double weight hanging from his wrists. Wrists and shoulders were aching horribly. But that was a pain, also, which he had learned to endure at sea. The sharp edges of the rock, here and there, bit right through the flesh of his hands, blood ran freely down his arms from the cuts. But he accepted that as a mere nothing. If his hands were frayed to the tendons and the skeleton bones, he would still hold on.

He came to the end of the swaying, perilous journey. Underneath him, at the end of the long, declining crack, there should be a number of irregularities. The cliff shelved out a trifle toward the bottom, and, in fact, he presently put his foot on a perfectly flat surface of stone. There he stood, his head turned, his chest against the rock, waiting for his breath to come back and for the shuddering fatigue to go out of his muscles.

He was far down now. When he raised his head, he saw both lips of the gorge inclining toward one another and the edges of the cliffs fencing an irregular road through the sky with the bright, yellow eye of Arcturus staring down at him, and he remembered what he had told the girl. There was a vast reassurance in that eye of light, a sort of personal recognition, as though it had knowledge of him, down there on the face of the slippery rock.

He started on again. He was down so far now that the thundering of the water had multiplied. The falling masses of water, not far from him, struck the roots of the cliff resounding, hurrying blows, and palpably shook it. And the darkness was infernal. It was better to close his eyes and trust to his hands, which felt and fumbled. He pulled off his boots and then in his bare feet secured better holds.

He came now to a broader ledge – perhaps four feet wide – and he was puzzled, because he could not remember having seen such a projection when he had looked down from the top of the cliff. Putting his hand out on the other side of it, he plunged his arm into swiftly running water. He had reached the footpath of the trail along the bottom of the rock!

He looked up at the ragged face of danger down which he had descended. Awe overwhelmed him. A new sense of dignity and of self-respect dropped upon Tom Derry out of the very sky. Strangely enough, it was not for two or three breathless seconds that he remembered the girl who waited in her agony at the top of the rock. Then he found a match and struck it.

In the cup of his two hands he lifted the light and moved it here and there. The flame burned to his flesh. He dropped that match and stared up. Had she seen? While he stared up, another thin and flickering point of fire bloomed and failed on the top of the rock. As it went out, it seemed to Tom Derry that the girl had spoken, had in physical presence appeared beside him.

He turned and hurried up the rocky trail. He passed the mouth of the gorge and came out on the wider valley beyond. The sense of peril still reached at him like a hand. It was not till he had gone a little distance under the bright arch of the stars that his nerves stopped jerking at his heart by a thousand little wires, and he was able to lift his head and walk upright, instead of cowering along like a hunted man.

It would not be far, now, to the place where Silver and Taxi were camped. Something, it seemed to him, slithered through the starlight ahead of him and disappeared among the brush. Might that not be Frosty, the wolf, scouting around the camp of his master?

Then, distinctly, he heard a low whinny. He stood still, and almost immediately the voice of Jim Silver called.

"Who's there?" he demanded.

"Your bad penny has turned up again. It's Derry," said the voice of Taxi.

"Come in, Derry," said Silver.

So Tom Derry walked forward through the denseness of brush and so into a cramped little clearing. A ray of light from Taxi's pocket torch cut across his face, across his body, and ended by wavering over his hands, and then dropped to his feet.

"Blood on his hands and bare feet," said Taxi. "He's had a go at something and he's been licked."

Derry raised his hands and pointed.

"Up there on the rocks are twenty men who are planning to get you, Silver, The Carys, and Christian, and Buck Rainey, and Stan Parker. They're waiting there to gather you in!"

The torch ray rose with a jerk and centred on his eyes till he blinked. Silver struck down that searching light.

"Be sensible, Taxi," he commanded. "I told you Derry was honest. Bleeding men don't tell lies like that."

"If there are twenty men up there, how did they happen to let you get away?" asked Taxi.

"They didn't let me. But there's a woman along with them. She cut the wires away from my wrists, and then I was able to

242

climb down the side of the gorge and get——"

"Wait a minute," commanded Taxi. "You climbed down the face of that cliff?"

"I did," said Derry. Then his anger rose and mastered him. "But it's not for your hide that I made the climb. I came to warn Silver not you!"

"It's a bluff and a sham," declared Taxi. "I don't think that a human being—— Let's see the inside of your hands, will you?"

Derry held them out, and the light wavered over the torn fingers.

Suddenly Taxi said: "Partner, I'm sorry. Crooked rats have made us trouble enough, and Silver will believe a lie, fast enough to make a man's head swim! But there's truth written all over your hands."

"There's truth written in more than his hands. How soon will they come this way, Derry? Taxi, you're better than a doctor, and you have the stuff in your saddle-bag. I have a pair of moccasins to cover your feet, Derry. How soon will they come, or can you guess?"

"After moonrise," said Derry. "After they've swallowed the pack train on the north side of the gulch."

"What pack train?" asked Silver.

"Men from down Wool Creek. They've been panning gold at the old diggings. They found a new streak and washed it right out. They've got a fortune on the backs of their mules, and at moonrise, the Carys are going to rush their camp."

Taxi had brought his medicaments and prepared to work on the hands of Derry.

"We've got to get through the gorge and warn those poor devils," said Silver.

"It's no good," answered Derry. "By this time Old Man Cary has two or three men with rifles plugging the gorge. You can't get through. They could stop an army in that place."

"We've got to try to unplug the gorge and get through, anyway. What people are those fellows with the gold?" asked Silver.

"Tenderfeet having a vacation in the mountains. Silver, you can't get through the gorge. I know, because I've just come out of it. The ledge the trail runs on is no more than a yard wide, part of the way, and those Carys will have their ears open, and be watching. You can't break a way through. I'm sure of that."

"How many of the tenderfeet are there?"

"A dozen."

"Armed?"

"Yes."

"Armed men, with gold in their packs, and that means they're sure to fight, and that means they're sure to die," said Silver. "Taxi, will you try to get through, with me?"

Taxi, working swiftly over the hands of Derry, cleansing them and then bandaging the fingers with rapid interlacing of cloth, snarled:

"Ask me whether I *want* to go, or not! Don't ask whether I will." Then, standing up from his work, as he finished the hands of Derry, he added: "We'd better start fast, Jim. Moonrise is only minutes away. What do we do with the horses?"

"If we can get through, we'll open a way for Parade, and he'll lead your horse, Taxi. Or, if it's safer to leave them here, Derry will stay with them."

"Me?" cried Derry, startled. "Stay here? I go with you, Silver!"

"Hello," said Taxi. "Is there another man started down the Silver road to trouble? Have you put the mischief into another poor devil of a man, Jim?"

"Your hands are badly used up. You'd better stay here, Derry," said Silver.

"Maybe I'd let the tenderfeet go hang," said Derry, "but I told you about the girl who cut the wires off my wrists. When I got down the cliff, I lighted a match to let her know that I was safe. But a match light isn't all she wants to see. I'm going with you, Silver."

Silver, for a moment, said nothing. It was Taxi who finally murmured:

"You've read a man right at last, Jim, have you? Well, I'm sorry for it, because, after this, you'll trust your judgment every time, and your judgment is always that men are honest. Derry, because you turn out a white man, you're shortening Jim's life for him!"

25

Frosty's Fangs

Taxi's horse they left behind them. Parade they brought along, to the surprise of Derry, but not until the hoofs of the great horse had been carefully muffled in soft wrappings of leather. When they came to the entrance of the gorge, they paused, and Silver put a hand on the shoulder of Taxi and the shoulder of Derry.

He said: "I'm going first, with Frosty ahead of me. He's been our lead horse more than once, and he's going to lead again tonight. You come after me, Taxi. Derry follows, and Parade will crowd you a little, because he'll want to get close to me. We don't know where we'll find the gorge blocked with the Carys. Frosty will find them for us. It's going to be dark in there, but not too dark for shooting, I suppose. That means we have to upset them before they have a look at us. And after Frosty has found them for us, I think he might upset them, too. If he does, I want you to remember that when it comes to close quarters, clubbed guns are apt to be better than bullets."

"Jim," said Taxi mournfully, "are you trying to spare the blood again? They're waiting ready to shoot us full of holes. Are you going to tie our right hands behind our backs before we go after them?"

"Even if they were wild Indians," said Silver, "there's no need to do more than our own safety calls for. The chances are that Frosty will fail. In that case, we'll have a shower of lead to walk through – and that means we have to shoot as fast and straight as we know how. But luck may help us though. I feel luck in the air, just now!"

They entered the gorge in the single file which Silver had indicated. To Derry, as he went watchfully along, the movements of the men were not particularly worth noticing; and even Frosty was not particularly to be wondered at as he scouted ahead. Any good dog could have been taught to do the same, perhaps. But Parade astonished Derry, for the great horse moved like a hunting cat, stealthily, putting down his feet with care, bending his knees to make the shock of the hoof fall

248

less. And when Derry turned and saw those shimmering eyes of the stallion by the starlight, he felt, in fact, that they could not fail, but that Silver had harnessed together uncanny power of dumb creation to work his will.

They went more than half-way down the ravine without the slightest pause, but where the waterfall lunged suddenly over a twenty-foot drop and hurled spray three times that height into the air, Silver halted the procession.

He drew Derry and Taxi close to him and shouted in their ears above the thunder of the falling water:

"Frosty's found something, and it must be men. I can tell by the way he's acting. They're down there at the foot of the fall somewhere, waiting. Taxi, you have the eyes of a cat and you can see in the dark. Go take a look. Be careful, but see what you can."

Taxi, accordingly, went forward, and Derry waited at the side of Silver for a few moments, feeling the wet of the spray settling on his hair and his face.

Then Taxi returned.

"They're down there," he said, "but they're covered up behind rocks. I saw one

249

man move. I got a glimpse of his head and shoulders. That was all. They're down there in cover. We've got to get over a twenty-foot drop of rock that slopes so fast you could almost slide on it. Jim, there's no use going ahead. They're able to blow the tar out of a hundred men, as fast as the hundred show their heads. This way is blocked!"

"I think I know how to unblock it," answered Silver. "It's a savage way, but we've got savages against us. Follow on close behind me, but not too close."

He made a gesture, and Frosty came to his feet.

"Let him smell the blood on your hands, Derry," directed Silver.

Derry held out his hands, and saw the shimmering white fangs of Frosty as the wolf crouched and snarled savagely. Then Silver kneeled by the wolf, talking to him words that Derry could not understand.

After that, he took Frosty gradually forward until they were close to the edge of the rock. For a moment, even in the dimness of the starlight, Silver could be seen restraining the great wolf by the ruff of his mane. When he loosed the animal, it was like letting go of a stone at the edge of a cliff. Frosty leaped over the edge of the declivity. An instant later, Silver waved his long arm to the others, and followed the way down the sloping rock.

Derry had received a revolver from Silver before they started to march. He had no chance to use it, however, for as he lurched, staggering down the sharp descent of the rock, he saw three men springing up before the furious assault of Frosty, and even above the roaring of the cataract, Derry could hear the screaming voices that shouted:

"Mad wolf! Mad wolf!"

They saw the charging form of Jim Silver then, and turned and fled, throwing their rifles this way and that.

The thing was over in a moment. The shrilling whistle of Silver called back Frosty. Three disarmed Carys were racing down the gorge – and the way had been cleared.

The three men – Silver, Taxi, and Derry – took it at a run, and came out into the open of the wider valley beyond.

They could see the three shadowy forms of the fleeing men leaping before them, head and shoulders against the stars. They could see, in the east, the brightening pyramid of light that announced the rising of the moon, and directly in front of it was the huddle of shadows that was the camp of the tenderfeet. At that same time, from this side and that of the encampment, out of the rocks and the shrubbery that surrounded it and under the bright eye of the rising moon itself, shadows of men sprang out, yelling like fiends.

Silver turned, flung himself into the saddle of Parade, and raced the horse forward, firing into the air as he went, shouting in a tremendous voice. And after him ran Derry and Taxi, firing in the same way into the air.

In the camp there was a wild tumult at once, but that rear charge was too much for the Carys, fighting men though they were.

Those directly in front of Silver's advance split to the right and to the left, yelling that they were sold. They ran with wings on their heels. The panic spread. That rush which should have wiped out the tenderfeet in a welter of blood turned into a mere ghostly gesture of danger that recoiled; and those wild men of the mountains swiftly were lost in the brush and the rocks. Their shouting and the occasional sound of gunfire were all that remained of the danger.

It had been finished in so brief a time that Derry was hardly in the camp before there was no further need of guns.

The moon came up in its full brightness to show those frightened gold-miners the termination of a scene that should have been the end of them.

They were not all tenderfeet, at that, for one grizzled old fellow who leaned on a long rifle in the middle of the encampment, where the fire had been built the evening before, said to the rest of the crew:

"Keepin' ward and watch was what I been preachin' to you, and keepin' ward and watch was what I was doin' when them scalawags jumped out of the brush yellin' their heads off. But one gun in one pair of hands wasn't no good agin' them. And before the rest of you had got the sleep out of your eyes, you'd 'a' been dead men. You'd 'a' been with the angels, my lads. And then come Jim Silver out of the gorge, and Parade leggin' it toward us, and then these other two, here. Like three wolves after a pack of hound dogs, and you can hear them hound dogs still howlin' and yappin', and brawlin' off there in the night!"

Those startled miners gathered with awe around their rescuers, but Derry was already gripping the arm of Silver and saying:

"Leave part of them here to guard their camp. Ask the rest of them to come with us, Jim. Up yonder I left the girl who gave us all the chance we had to do this. Will you ask them to ride with us, Jim?"

Ride with their saviours?

They yelled their pleasure. Saddles were jerked on to the backs of horses. In two minutes they were under way, with Derry thumping the ribs of an earnest little mustang as he strove vainly to catch up with the mighty, bounding strides of Parade.

So they stormed over the slope and over the edge of plateau. Here and there they searched, and the voice of Derry rang with agony as he called for Molly.

But all they could find of the Cary encampment were a few scattered and forgotten articles of clothing. The men were gone, and with them they had taken Molly. She was nowhere to be found.

Up there in the ragged mass of the mountains, perhaps, they were hurrying her along. And who could follow through

the naked rocks over which the clan
fleeing?

Silver gripped the shoulder of Derry.

"There are three of us, and Frosty," he
said. "We can't expect the rest of these men
to go. Numbers will never catch that outfit,
anyway. But we'll hang on their trail till
they can wish that they had wings to get
away from us!"

26

The Pursuit

It was arranged and started before the gold hunters had a chance to be well aware of what was happening. Whatever thanks they had to offer went unspoken, for the only thing that Silver asked was two saddled horses. They were his as soon as he had spoken. Down the valley, beyond the gorge, the tenderfeet were told, they would find Taxi's horse – and keep it until called for.

Then the three men, with Frosty to guide them faultlessly on the way, entered the great rock wilderness of the mountain summits. They had the moon to help them, but the same moon was up there to help the Cary marksmen. The hat was lifted off Jim Silver's head by one well-directed shot. Another cut through the shirt of Derry, under the pit of his arm. But most of the time they managed to keep to shelter, while pressing in.

256

Now and again they saw dim forms pelting away from one rear post to another.

Why do twenty men let three drive them, was the question in the mind of Derry. But one of the three was Silver, and even Barry Christian did not have money or persuasion enough to send the Carys back to face the rifle of Silver. Or perhaps Christian was no longer with the crew. That failure of the raid may have induced them to throw him off, and he, with an angling flight, might be working away in another direction through the uplands, while the Carys brought after them the effects of the attempt.

In the pink of the dawn, they were well above timber line and passing through a rolling plateau covered with mosses and lichens more than with grass. Small lakes lay here and there, looking up to the sky with far bluer eyes than the colour they were drinking up in return. And as they approached a badlands of broken rock again, Derry saw a woman sitting on a stone at the edge of a little creek.

She sat with her hands clasped around one knee, the posture of a man. Her arms were bare to the shoulders. When she turned her head, he could see the long gleam of the dark, braided hair that fell down her back.

He waved an arm and tried to shout. His voice slowly died in his throat.

Then: "Molly!" he thundered, and drove the mustang into a frantic gallop.

She waited till he was almost up to her before she got up from the stone. She was neither laughing nor weeping. She was as calm as the mountains around her when he flung himself from the back of the bronco and caught hold of her.

Something that was not indifference, but as quiet looked up at him from her eyes.

"The old man turned me loose," she said. "Some of 'em wanted to hang me up by the hair of my head, because I'm a traitor. But the old man said it wasn't to be. He told me to tell you that I'm a present to you, and the devil with you, he said."

"Molly, you don't care a whole heap, it looks like," said Derry.

"Don't I? said she. "Well, if you'll finish off mauling me around, your friends can stop pretending that they've got saddle girths to tighten. They can come on up. And I want to meet Jim Silver. I want to look him in the face."

She looked at Derry and added: "And now that you've got me, what are you going

258

to do with me?"

"How old are you, Molly?" he asked.

"I'm not quite twenty," she answered.

"How much is 'quite'?"

"Oh, a year or so."

"Molly, cross your heart to die if you're more than – than – " He hesitated, staring closely into her eyes. "By the leaping thunder, you're not more than sixteen years old. Tell me I'm a liar if you dare!"

She said nothing. Trouble came into her eyes.

"It isn't the years that matter," she said. "It's the kind of years that really count. Now you've hounded the Carys – you and your Jim Silver – into turning me out of the clan, what are you going to do with me, Tom?"

"I'm going to send you to school," said he grimly. "You can stand some teaching, I guess."

"Maybe the school will learn something, too," said Molly.

He stared at her again. Wonder began to grow in him that she had told him the truth about her age, and that she had accepted his decision for her future.

"Molly," he said, "how do you feel?"

"Sort of still and quiet," she said. "How

would you feel if you had twenty men in your family one minute, and only one the next?"

The publishers hope that this book has given you enjoyable reading. Large Print Books are specially designed to be as easy to see and hold as possible. If you wish a complete list of our books, please ask at your local library or write directly to: John Curley & Associates, Inc. P.O. Box 37, South Yarmouth Massachusetts, 02664